Zane & Lucky's First Christmas
(Forever Love)

J. S. Cooper

Thank you for purchasing a J. S. Cooper book!
Join my
MAILING LIST
to be notified of new releases and teasers!

Copyright

This book is a work of fiction. Any resemblance to actual persons, living or dead, or actual events is entirely coincidental. Names, characters, businesses, organizations, places, events, and incidents are either the product of the author's imagination or are used fictitiously.

Table of Contents

Chapter 1

Zane

"Imagine yourself floating in the ocean. Go on and close your eyes, everyone." The instructor's voice was soft, and I followed her command with pleasure. I had been ready to close my eyes as soon as she started showing us charts and photos of the labor process. I wanted to burn the images from my mind. I'd tried to look away, but Lucky had pinched me and given me a look. "Now imagine that you are surrounded by warm calming water. And think nice pleasurable thoughts. Think of your loved one. Think of how much fun it's going to be when you bring your little one home. And just keep thinking those thoughts."

I lay back with my eyes closed and imagined Lucky and I playing in the backyard with Skylar and Noah. Lucky would be playing with the kids, while Noah and I grilled burgers and hot dogs. I paused as I thought about the scene—something was missing. I thought for a moment, and then I added Robin to the image in my mind. Lucky and Robin would be playing with the kids, while Noah and I grilled. I smiled as I pictured myself grabbing Lucky and sneaking her upstairs to the bedroom for a quickie, while Robin and Noah looked after the kids. That would be hot and needed. I was already worried about how much sex Lucky and I would be having after she had the babies. The doctor had said that it could be months before Lucky would be able to and wanted to have sex. I wasn't sure she had appreciated me asking him that question, but I'd wanted to know.
"Are you feeling calm?" Her voice sounded soothing, and I felt myself drifting off. This class wasn't so bad after all. The floor wasn't super comfortable, but I suppose beggars couldn't be choosers. I wasn't sure why I had been so loath to come with Lucky, this was really not bad at all. I was imagining what Lucky was going to do to me tonight to thank me for coming with her when someone starting screaming loudly.
"What the fuck?" I shouted as I sat forward, blinking rapidly as I looked around the room. There were several couples looking at me in distaste, and one stuck-up looking redhead was shaking her head at me. I could almost hear her thoughts. "He's going to be a bad dad," she was thinking. I looked at Lucky and she glared at me and I gave her a

1

lopsided grin. "Oops, sorry everyone." I apologized to the instructor and she gave me a small patient smile.

"That's okay, Mr. Beaumont. Now you know what your babies are thinking, folks. The birthing process is just as tedious for them as it is for you. They are calm, warm, enjoying the comfort of their mother's belly and then all of a sudden they are pushed into the world, and it is cold, bright, loud and scary. If they could speak, it is very likely that they would also be saying some variation of 'what the fuck' as well." She smiled wickedly at me and I laughed. I looked around the room again, as if to say I'm not the only one, but no one else was laughing. The redhead looked madder than ever, and her husband looked like he wanted to run away and hide. I wanted to tell him to get out of dodge, but I guess it was too late. He'd already gotten her pregnant. I shivered for him as I realized that he was going to have to spend the rest of his life with someone that looked like she was having a colonoscopy every second of the day.

"I am going to kill you, Zane," Lucky whispered to me when the instructor gave us a few minutes to gather our thoughts.

"It's not my fault." I shrugged. "She scared me."

"How could she have scared you?"

"I was sle…I mean, I was thinking happy thoughts about our babies and next thing I know someone is screaming like they are being murdered. I thought someone was giving birth in the room or something."

"That's the point." She rolled her eyes. "She was simulating what the birthing process is like for the baby. Giving birth is hard for the mother and for the babies."

"I know," I said, feeling very serious all of a sudden. "I'm sorry, Lucky."

"It's okay." She reached over and squeezed my hand. "It was kind of funny."

"Do you think everything's going to be okay?" I looked into her eyes. "When you give birth and everything?"

"It's going to be fine."

"Are you sure they gave you all the tests?" I could hear the worry in my voice. "We can get you to some new doctors if you don't trust the information you've received so far."

"I trust my doctor, Zane," she said patiently.

"Are you sure? We need to make sure that you don't—"

"Everything is going to be fine, Zane." She reached over and kissed me on the cheek. "I know you're worried, but everything is going to be fine."

"I'm just scared, after hearing about my mom, you know."

"I know." She nodded and jumped up. "I understand."

"Okay, everyone. The break is done. Who's ready for some fun?" The instructor spoke loudly and the room fell silent. She looked around waiting for someone to answer, and I stuck my hand up.

"I'm ready," I spoke up, and I saw the redhead give me an annoyed look out of the corner of my eye. "I'm very ready," I continued, laughing to myself. "Is there a room that Lucky and I can go into?" I continued, deliberately misunderstanding what she had meant. "I didn't know we were going to practice how to make a baby as well."

"Zane." Lucky grabbed my arm, the red rising in her face.

"I'm sorry, Mr. Beaumont, but that is not the type of fun I was talking about." The instructor gave me a small frown, but I could see a glimpse of humor in her eyes. I was pretty sure she was glad to have people like Lucky and me in her classes, along with the stuck up bitches from Beverly Hills.

"Oh, darn." I laughed and put my arm around Lucky's waist. "I guess it's obvious we don't have a problem in that department. We're having twins." Lucky pinched my waist hard, and she glared at me again as I looked at her.

"I am going to kill you when we get home. You're in so much trouble."

"Going to spank me, are you?" I whispered back and she laughed as she rolled her eyes.

"You wish. Now, shh."

"If you two are done, I would like to continue on with our next session." The instructor gave us a disapproving look, along with the rest of the class, and I realized we were the bad apples in the class. I knew that Noah would think it was funny as hell when I told him what happened. That would teach Lucky to bring me along to these things. She knew I had no interest in watching videos of women giving birth and screaming. What man really wanted to see all that? I mean, it was a good video for a sex education class: it would stop boys from sleeping around, possibly. But it sure wasn't doing anything for me, as a soon-to-be father.

"Right now, husbands and boyfriends, and of course, girlfriends, I want you to practice supporting your partner. When they are in the delivery room, they're going to be in pain. They're going to be worried. They're going to be scared. They're going to need your support in multiple ways. Now, does anyone know what actions you can take to support your partner?"

"We can hold her hand," a big biker dude spoke up. "So she can squeeze it hard when she pushes."

"That's what she said," I whispered to Lucky, but she ignored me.

"Yes," the instructor said. "Handholding is very important. But do not force her to hold your hand if she doesn't want to. Also, realize that if she is squeezing your hand hard, it is not a good idea to complain about the pressure. If you don't think you can deal with it without complaining, it might be a better idea to get her a stress toy to squeeze."

"She can hold my hand anytime." The biker dude grinned. "I'm a strong dude. I can take it." I looked at him, and laughed inside. I bet he was going to be the first one to faint in the delivery room, once his wife started pushing. It was always the ones that looked rough and tough that were the wussiest ones.

"Any other ideas, guys? What can you do to support your partner?"

"You can tell her how beautiful she is." The redhead's husband spoke up and she smiled at him appreciatively.

"Yes, you can do that." The instructor nodded and I rolled my eyes. What woman wanted to hear she was beautiful as she pushed a basketball out of her vagina? "Anything else?" She looked around and the class was quiet. I noticed that all the other guys were either staring at their feet or the wall, and looked as bored as I felt.

"Okay, guys." The instructor laughed. "I guess I'll take it from here. You can also rub your wife's feet. There are pressure points in her feet that will help her loosen up and relax while in labor."

"I like feet." One skinny man spoke up eagerly. "I can do that."

"That's good." The instructor gave him a quick smile. "What we're all going to do now is practice rubbing our partner's feet."

"Now?" I looked over at her and frowned. "I thought the class was done in two minutes?"

"No, Mr. Beaumont. There is no official end time to the class. It all depends on when we get through everything we need to do."

"Okay," I frowned. "But the class schedule says the class ends at 7 p.m."

"Well, as I just told you, it's not yet ending, Mr. Beaumont." All humor was gone from her face. "Everyone go back to your mats, please. And we will practice making our partners comfortable with a foot rub. Remember, husbands, this is not about you. You are not the ones going through the pain of delivery. You are not the ones giving birth. Your job is to make your partner happy and as relaxed as possible. You have to be patient." She gave me a look, and then turned around and walked over to her small boom box. "Now, I'm going to play some music that can be soothing in stressful situations."

"I wonder if she's going to play Kanye West." I whispered to Lucky as we sat down.

"Yes, Zane, she's going to start blasting 'Golddigger'," Lucky grinned at me, and slapped me in the arm. "You're going to get us kicked out, you know."

"No, I'm not. I haven't done anything bad." I shook my head innocently.

"You're acting like an idiot." She shook her head with a half-smile. "I should be so mad at you."

"You're not?" I tilted my head to the side.

"How could I be mad at you?" She laughed. "But you better believe I'm going to be squeezing the shit out of your hand."

"Ooh, you just said shit." I laughed at her and she blushed.

"We're seriously going to be the worst mom and dad." She laughed. "Our kids are going to get kicked out of preschool for cursing."

"Not with Uncle Noah in the picture." I grinned. "He will school us."

"True," she laughed. "He's taken to fatherhood like a fish to water."

"Yeah, he has." I smiled and warmth filled my heart as I thought about Noah and Skylar and how close they were. I never would have believed that Noah would be a dad in his early twenties, and to see him in the role made me see him in a new and even more respectful light. My brother really was the best man I knew.

"Maybe I should have brought him here with me."

"Are you trying to make me jealous?" I pulled her to me and she giggled as I kissed her neck. "He may be my brother, but that doesn't mean I wouldn't slap him silly if he even thought about getting close to you."

"Zane, you're an idiot." Lucky's eyes shined brightly into mine. "He's my brother as well, and he has Robin."

"Well, we hope he has Robin." I made a face, suddenly feeling sad for Noah. They had agreed to start over again, but Robin really didn't seem to have much time for him. I wasn't positive that she was going to get over the secrets he had kept from her, and that made me feel bad for him. I knew just how much he really liked her.

"Well, if it doesn't work out with Robin, he can always see if he likes Leeza. She's coming to visit in a few months."

I groaned at the mention of her friend's name. I wanted nothing to do with Leeza and, frankly, I was pissed that Lucky was still friends with her. "Leeza will never date my brother." I shook my head. "No way do I want a tramp in my family."

"She's not a tramp." Lucky glowered at me.

"How's it going, you two?" The instructor walked up to us. "Now is the time to connect as partners having a baby. Small talk can be had after the class."

"Yes, sorry." Lucky sat back and blushed. "Stop distracting me, Zane."

"Or?"

"You're going to have us kicked out."

"You really think so?"

"Yes!"

"We're going to get kicked out for talking?" I mumbled to myself and sat in front of her and slid her shoes off. She placed her feet on my lap and sat back. Her long dark hair hung in curls down her back, and she closed her eyes as she relaxed. I took her right foot in my hand and started caressing it. She smiled at me as she relaxed and I stared at her, feeling the love surge through me. Her other foot nudged closer to my crotch and I wondered if she was trying to tease me. I grinned as I thought of a way to really relax Lucky. I'd show her how to get kicked out of the class, I thought to myself. "How does this feel?" I asked her softly as I kneaded the soles of her feet.

"Good." She moaned, and slowly opened up her eyes to stare at me. Her lips looked pink and lush and from my vantage point, she looked sexy as hell. I felt a stirring in my pants and I shifted slightly as her foot rested itself and pressed into my crotch. She grinned at me as I moved her foot and I realized she had been doing it on purpose. I smiled back at her and grinned to myself. *Just wait, Lucky,* I laughed inside. She lay back and closed her eyes again and I started kneading her foot again. Then I quickly lifted it to my mouth and bent my head and took her big toe in my mouth and starting sucking it. I made a big deal of sucking it and really enjoying it. Within seconds, Lucky had sat upright in shock and there were several gasps from around the class.

"Zane," she blushed as she pulled her foot away from me. "What are you doing?"

"Excuse me, you two." The instructor hurried over to us. "I'm afraid I'm going to have to ask you to leave. This class is for couples looking to make the delivery process easier. It's not for those interested in public sex displays."

"What?" Lucky gasped and I could see from her face that she was mortified. "That's not why we're here."

"Come on, Honey. I guess we came to the wrong class." I jumped up and grinned.

"No, we didn't. This is the…" Lucky started and I grabbed her hand. "This is the class for the up-tight parents, not the cool and fun, 'we're still going to fuck every night' parents." I grinned and stared at the redhead's husband, who was looking at me with jealousy. "Let's go home."

"Oh my God, Zane. I'm going to kill you." Lucky whispered to me, as we hurried out of the class. All the women were looking at Lucky in sympathy, but all the men were looking at me in jealousy. Poor suckers.

"Thank God." I breathed the fresh air in, as we walked out of the building. "I thought I was going to suffocate in there."

"What the fuck did you just do?"

"Now, now, Mommy-to-be. Are you sure you want our babies to hear that language?" I looked at her with a shocked expression and she hit me in the arm.

"You're an asshole."

"But you love me."

"Zane, that was a serious class. You can't do that stuff."

"Lucky, that class was a bunch of bull. I thought I was in a horror movie at one point when the screaming started." She shook her head and looked at me wordlessly as I continued. "And did you see the miserable faces of everyone else in the class? It was depressing."

"It was a bit depressing." She smiled slowly. "But, you were still out of order."

"Did you really want to go back and hang out with those women? Did you really want to be a part of their mommy-and-me groups?"

"No," She laughed reluctantly. "Okay, okay, you're right. They sucked." She sighed. "Let's just go home."

"Don't be mad at me." I made a face as we walked to the car. "Don't leave me for my brother."

"Idiot, if I leave you it won't be for another goofy overprotective Beaumont, it will be for some hot stud." She grinned at me, and then ran away as I tried to grab her.

"You better not even be thinking about any hot studs." I felt a knife twist in my gut at the thought of Lucky daydreaming about some other man.

"Then you better not mess around in the next class we attend." She gave me a look as we got to my car.

"What? We have to go to another class?" I sighed.

"We didn't really learn anything tonight, aside from the fact that you're a smart ass."

"You knew that already."

"Oh, and that you have a foot fetish." Lucky shook her head, trying to stop herself from laughing.

"You weren't exactly saying no." I grinned as I started the car and winked at her. "And your foot was certainly telling me what you were thinking!"

"What are you talking about?"

"Your foot was caressing me." I raised an eyebrow at her and she frowned.

"What?"

"You were teasing my cock with your foot." I grinned at her. "Trying to get me turned on, huh?"

"Zane, I have no idea what you're talking about. If my foot accidentally hit your crotch it was by mistake. I certainly wasn't trying to turn you on in a pregnancy class."

"Oh," I laughed. "My bad."

"Oh my gosh." She laughed. "You're too much." She sighed and looked at me with a loving gaze. "I love you, Zane, but sometimes you're just too much."

"Sorry." I laughed, happy that we could tease each other and have moments like this without her getting all angry and serious. "Shall we pick up some ice cream for Skylar?"

"I don't think so." She paused. "It's a bit late. I'm sure she'll be in bed. And I don't think it's good to give kids sugar late at night."

"I think that's just Coke and Pepsi," I said, as if I actually had a clue.

"I'm pretty sure it's sugar stuff as well." Lucky made a face.

"I guess we should look it up."

"Or we could go to a pregnancy class." Lucky reached over and rested her head on my shoulder. "That may be the best bet."

"I guess so," I conceded and groaned inside. How many more gory videos and loud-pitched screams was I going to have to deal with? I paused as I realized that it could be a lot worse. Lucky could be having a difficult pregnancy and we could be worried about her life, or the lives of the babies. All things considered, I guessed going to a pregnancy class wasn't as bad as it got.

◉≫

"Skylar, it's time for bed." Noah was standing by the stairs when we got home, with his hands on his hips. "You have to go up now."

"I'm watching something." Skylar called back to him, without moving her eyes away from the TV.

"Hey, Bro," I grinned at my brother as we walked through the door. "Good night?"

"A trying night." He shook his head. "Skylar, if you don't get off the couch, there will be no TV tomorrow night."

"That's not fair!" She cried out, and looked up. Then she spotted me and Lucky, and broke into a smile before jumping off of the couch and running over to us. "Uncle Zane and Aunty Lucky are home, yay!" She ran into my arms and I picked her up and swung her around.

"You being a good girl?" I sat her down and gave her a serious look.

"Yes." She nodded and grinned up at me. "I'm always a good girl."

"You know that Santa Claus only comes for good girls." I continued on talking. "In fact, if you're a bad girl, the Grinch will come and he'll take away—"

"Zane," Lucky grabbed my arm and squeezed. "I think that's enough."

"Huh?" I looked back at her and then realized that perhaps I was going a bit too far with my story. "Well, just be a good girl, Skylar, and listen to what Noah says." She looked up at me with a confused expression.

"Is Santa coming?" Her lower lip started trembling, and I felt my stomach churning. Uh, oh I've gone and screwed this up. "I've been good. I promise."

"I think Santa is going to have a conversation with Noah in a few months and then will decide if he's going to come." I smiled at her gently and then saw Noah trying not to laugh at me. "So you better go and get ready for bed now."

"Okay, Uncle Zane." She nodded and gave me a small hug. "Night night, Aunty Lucky."

"Night, my precious." She gave Skylar a kiss on the cheek, and then Skylar went running over to Noah.

"I'm ready to go to bed now, Noah."

"Okay, run upstairs and brush your teeth and I'll come and tuck you in when you're done."

"Okay." She grinned and ran up the stairs. "I want a goodnight story as well."

"We'll see."

"Please, Noah." She paused on the stairs and looked back down with pleading eyes. "I really want to read tonight."

"Go and brush your teeth, and we'll see." He grinned up at her and then walked over to us, once she had gone back up the stairs.

"Long night?" I laughed as I looked at his tired expression.

"You do not even know." He yawned. "She didn't want to eat fish sticks, she didn't want to drink apple juice. She wanted ice cream for dessert and then when she got ice cream, she wanted cake. And then when she got cake, she wanted chocolate. And then when she got chocolate she spat it out and wanted the ice cream again." He took a deep breath. "So yeah, it was a long night."

"You're doing a good job, Noah." Lucky squeezed his arm.

"Yeah, he's doing a good job at letting her have whatever she wants for dessert." I laughed. "Can we say that she's totally pulling all the strings?"

"Whatever." Noah walked over to the couch and flopped down. "Just wait until you have kids."

"I know I'll be loving but firm." I sat on the couch next to him.

"Zane, you don't even have the patience for a pregnancy class." Lucky laughed at me. "I don't know that you're going to be Super Dad right off the bat."

"That class sucked." I gave her a grin. "Trust me, once the babies arrive I'll be fine."

"What temperature do their bottles need to be?" she questioned me, raising an eyebrow.

"What bottle?" I asked in confusion.

"The bottle with their formula." She smiled at me gently.

"Aren't you going to breastfeed them?" I couldn't stop myself from staring at her growing bosoms. "Why will they need formula?"

"I may not create enough milk for both of them, Zane. It's something we have to prepare for."

"Oh." I shrugged. "I guess you'll figure it out."

"No, Zane. I won't be figuring anything out. We will be figuring it out." She plopped down on my lap and grinned at me before giving me a quick kiss. "Remember what Nancy said, we're in this together and we have to make decisions together."

"Who's Nancy and when did she say this?" I was totally confused as to what Lucky was talking about.

"Oh my God, Zane." She jumped off of my lap and gave me a disapproving look. "Nancy was the instructor in our class tonight, and that was the first thing she said after we all introduced ourselves."

"Oh, yeah." I smiled up at her weakly. I had totally spaced out during that conversation and had been thinking about trying to find a way to ask Lucky if she wanted to talk about possibly getting married in Vegas. "Oh, yeah, my foot." Lucky shook her head. "You have no idea what she said, do you?" She glared at me. "I'm going upstairs to have a shower, and no, before you ask, I do not want to share it with you."

I watched as she walked up the stairs and sat back and sighed. "Guess that didn't go very well." I looked over at Noah who was trying very hard to keep a straight face.

"Yeah, I recommend you get your act together, Bro, or you may find that you're on Santa's naughty list this Christmas." He raised an eyebrow at me, and we both burst out laughing.

Chapter 2

Noah

"Which book would you like us to read tonight, Skylar?" I pulled the bed sheets and duvet over her before sitting down in the new armchair Lucky had bought for the room.

"Not *Goldilocks and the Three Bears*," she yawned, "or *Cinderella*. Something new."

"Okay," I laughed. "We can read something new." I stared at her face as she looked at me with wide eager eyes. A swell of love filled my heart as she looked up at me with an open and loving face. She had only been living here as my adopted daughter for a month, but I could already see a huge difference in her appearance and her demeanor. She was happy almost all of the time now. There were still times when I would see her thinking hard, and she looked downcast. Whenever I saw her looking too sad, I would go up to her and tickle her until she couldn't stop laughing, and then we would have a quick cuddle. "What about *The Jolly Postman?*"

"Yes, yes." She sat up eagerly. "I want to read it to you, please."

"I'd be happy for you to read it to me."

"Noah," she said my name slowly. "Do you ever think about Palm Bonita?"

"Sometimes." I smiled at her slowly, and my stomach lurched. So far, we hadn't really had any conversations about Monica, and I was worried that she was going to have a bad delayed reaction. Lucky had suggested that we go to a child therapist together to make sure that no issues developed, but I hadn't thought that was necessary. "Why?"

"I was just thinking about the day that we first met." She blinked at me. "Do you miss Monica?"

"No." I felt heat rise in my face. I could still remember the first time she had seen me, while I had been in bed with her stepmother. I was praying to God that she wasn't talking about that incident, but rather about the more formal introduction. "Do you?"

"Not really." She shook her head and bit her lip. "Does that make me a bad girl?"

"Of course not, sweetheart." I stared at her innocent nine-year-old face and felt tongue-tied. I really didn't know what to say. It wasn't like I could tell her that there was no way in hell I missed that bitch Monica and that no one would ever call her a bad girl for hating the witch. "Monica loved you in the best way that she could," I took a hold of her hand. "But she didn't really know how to love." *Anyone but herself.* "She loved you in her own way, but needed to take care of her own issues."

"I'm glad she left me with you." Skylar's eyes were wide and I could tell that she was trying not to cry. "She said that if you didn't give her money she was going to make things bad for you."

"Don't worry about what she said, Darling. She's gone from our lives forever." I pulled her towards me and stroked her hair. "We're a family now."

"You, me, Uncle Zane, Aunty Lucky, and the new babies." She grinned as she pulled away from me. "I can't wait to have brothers and sisters."

"They won't be your siblings." I laughed at her and pinched her cheek. "They'll be your cousins."

"Oh, okay, yeah. I can't wait to have cousins." She lay back in the bed and yawned again. "And then one day, I can have brothers and sisters as well."

"That would be nice, wouldn't it?"

"And a mommy." She closed her eyes and her words were slightly slurred. "I'd like to have a real mommy as well."

"I know, Darling." Robin's face flashed in my mind, and I felt a wave of sadness fill my soul. Nothing had been the same after the day I had left Robin's apartment to rush home without telling her what was going on. She had said that she was willing to move past everything and try again, but we'd only seen each other twice in the last month and both times had been awkward. Every night, I thought about her and making love to her. My body ached to touch her and be touched by her, but we hadn't slept with each other since that incident. I knew that she was hurt by what happened, but I wasn't sure what else I could do to get her to open herself up to me, and to give me a new chance. A real new chance. I sighed as I thought about the fact that Skylar was as far away from getting a mommy as I was from figuring out Robin. I was about to stand up and get the book when I realized that Skylar was sleeping. I looked down at her sweet face as she slept and gave her a quick kiss on the cheek before turning the light off and exiting the room.

13

I walked back down the stairs and into the kitchen to see if I could find something to eat, as I had forgotten to make myself something when Skylar had been acting up.

"That was quick," Zane looked up from the fridge as I entered the kitchen. "Want a beer?"

"Yeah, thanks." I nodded. "Skylar fell asleep already. Long day, I guess."

"I bet." Zane opened the bottles and handed me one. "Lucky was right, though, you're doing a great job."

"Thanks." I took a chug and sighed. "It's a lot harder than it looks." I opened a cupboard and looked for some chips. "Want to share a pizza?" I closed the cupboard door and walked over to the fridge.

"Sure." Zane grinned. "You call and I'll go ask Lucky what she wants on her slices."

"I thought she liked ham and onions?"

"She does," He rolled his eyes. "But she's on this thing about not assuming she wants what she wants."

"What?" I laughed, slightly confused.

"We all know she wants ham and onions on her pizza, but we can't order that until she says that's what she wants." He made a face at me. "I think it's the pregnancy brains, it's made her all crazy."

"Oh," I said, laughing.

"Don't get married, Bro. It will save you from many gray hairs."

"You're not married yet," I laughed. "You can always walk away and give a better guy a shot."

"Why do I feel you're not joking?" He half-smiled at me, and stared at me. "Everything okay with you and Robin?"

"There is no me and Robin." I looked away. "Go and get Lucky's permission and I'll call. You want pepperoni, peppers, onions and extra cheese, right?"

"You got it." He laughed. "I'll be right back. Why don't you give Robin a call and see if she wants to come over."

"She won't."

"Give her a call anyway. Just to see." He gave me a look. "If you like her, you'll need to pursue her a bit harder."

"I'm trying, she's just getting over what happened."

"Can you blame her? She let you into her life, into her bed and maybe into her heart and you held the biggest secrets you could from her."

"It wasn't because I wasn't falling for her." I said defensively. "In fact, she's the only girl I've felt that connected to."

"Does she know that?" He looked at me with a stern expression.

14

"I don't know." I sighed. "She doesn't care."

"Stop being so defeatist, Noah. I know you think you're the savior of the world and the keeper of all of mankind's secrets, but you're just a human like the rest of us. You do make mistakes, and while I know your heart does what you think is best, sometimes you get it wrong."

"Okay, tell it like it is." I made a face at Zane. "I know I fucked up. I just thought that...."

"Stop thinking already. I know what you thought, I'm sure Robin knows what you thought, but sometimes you have to think about what the other people are thinking as well."

"So I'm a screw-up, huh?"

"Basically." He laughed and punched me in the shoulder. "But I still love you. Just call her and see what happens. I'll be back after Lucky tells me what I already know."

"Okay, okay. I'll call." I turned away from him and pulled out my phone. I stared at it for a few seconds before pressing the numbers. I held my breath as it rang, and I could feel the disappointment seeping out of my pores as it kept ringing. I was about to hang up, when she answered.

"Hello," her voice was soft and my heart ached at the sound of it.

"Robin!" I said brightly and too eagerly. I stifled a groan.

"Hey."

"Hey." I answered and then there was a moment of silence. "How are you?"

"Fine."

"I tried calling you a few...."

"I was busy." She said abruptly.

"I see." I bit my lip, unsure of what to say next. "So Zane and I were about to order pizza and I was wondering if you would like to come over and share some with us."

"Really? It's 8pm." I could tell she was feeling feisty by the tone in her voice.

"Yeah, we're having a late dinner."

"Am I the dinner?"

"What?" I frowned into the phone.

"You call me out of the blue at 8pm at night and ask if I want to come over for dinner. And I want to know if I'm the dinner. Is this a booty call?"

"Of course it's...."

"Of course, if it is, you wouldn't tell me. I'd be the last one to know, right?"

"Robin, this is not a booty call." I sighed. "Honestly, I think a booty call would be if I had called you at midnight. And then I wouldn't ask you to come over for pizza."

"Oh, you'd ask me to come over for some dick."

"Uhm," I tried not to laugh. I knew that she hadn't intended to be funny, but for some reason I couldn't stop myself from finding her last statement really funny. "If you want to."

"What?" she screeched, and I knew she was surprised at what I had said. But I was too tired to mess around anymore. Either she liked me or she didn't. Either way, I wasn't going to play games.

"If you want to come over for some pizza, then that's fine. If you want to come over for some dick, preferably my dick, then that is also fine. Big Noah was talking to me the other day and he did tell me that he misses you, so I'm sure you would be very welcome."

"You're an asshole."

"I've been told that once or twice."

"You're possibly the biggest asshole I know." She continued.

"Big Noah just told me that he wouldn't mind exploring your asshole." I joked and the phone went silent. "Sorry, Robin. I didn't mean that. It was a bad joke. I have a problem of joking at the most inappropriate times."

"Yes, you do." Robin gasped and then burst out laughing and my heart soared with hope at the sound of her giggles.

"Let me make it up to you. Whatever you want on your pizza is all yours. I'll even buy you your own."

"I don't know." She hesitated.

"Please." I begged. "I miss you."

"I guess." She sighed. "But I'm not staying over."

"Fine." I grinned into the phone. "You don't have to stay over."

"Big Noah better not try and beg me." She laughed. "'Cause I'll tell him no, too."

"To his face?"

"You wish."

"More like he does." I shifted my legs as I felt big Noah awakening at the possibility of coming out for the night.

"Big Noah and small Noah both wish." She giggled. "Though, I don't know which one is in charge of the other."

"No fair." I groaned, because at that moment, I wasn't sure either.

"Anyways, I'm going to hang up now, so that you can come over before you change your mind."

"Scaredy-cat," she laughed. "I'm not a flake, you know."

"Uh huh."

"Okay, I'm just going to go brush my hair and I'll be over."

"Don't forget your toothbrush."

"What?"

"Nothing." I said quickly. "See you soon."

"Wait, Noah." She almost screamed into the phone.

"Yes." I held my breath, wondering if she had been playing me, trying to get my hopes up before changing her mind.

"Pepperoni and jalapenos please."

"Huh?"

"On the pizza."

"Oh, yeah," I laughed.

"There are going to be pizzas, right?"

"Of course." I answered quickly, hoping her mind didn't start jumping to conclusions.

"Okay, I guess—"

"I gotta go." I said hurriedly. "See you soon." And then I hung up. There was no way I was going to give her the option to change her mind. I stood there for a few minutes with a huge grin on my face and happiness in my heart as I realized that she was definitely coming. But that wasn't the reason for my thudding heart and hopeful mindset. That was because she had sounded like she was open to really giving me another chance to make it up to her. It was crazy that I cared about her so much; we barely knew each other, but I already felt so connected to her. I knew that if I didn't try to make things right with us, I would lose her. Scratch that, I needed to make things better than right. I needed her to give me a new chance, a fresh chance. Because I had a feeling that if she did that, things would work out for the best.

Ding dong. I ran to the door excitedly, only pausing to take a breath before I opened it nonchalantly.

"Hey," I smiled, expecting to see Robin on the other side of the door.

"Hey, Bro. What's up?" Leonardo's handsome mug grinned back at me before he reached over and gave me a brotherly hug.

"Leo," I hugged him back and tried not to show my disappointment. "How are you?"

"I'm good, but I want to hear everything." He stared at me and laughed. "Look at you all buff, I see you've been working out a lot more."

"Well, you know." I laughed as I let him in, and we walked to the living room. "There's not much to do when you're in hiding." I looked over at my brother's best friend and chuckled before becoming serious. "It was hard being away."

"I bet." He gave me a look. "We thought you were dead."

"I know."

"Zane was devastated."

"I know."

"Don't do it again." He gave me a look and I nodded, understanding his unspoken words. I had nearly killed my brother inside and out. It had been selfish of me to disappear and not say anything; I still thought my reasons were respectable, but as time went by, I was starting to see that I didn't have to be a martyr in the situation.

"So Zane got himself a hottie," Leo joked, breaking the tension in the room.

"I heard that, Leo." Zane came running down the stairs and into the living room. "Don't you go getting any thoughts into your head."

"Scared of a little competition?" Leo joked and Zane laughed.

"Never."

"If Lucky's a smart girl, I think we both know how this will end." Leo winked at Zane and I laughed.

"Yeah, she'll choose me." I joined the conversation and Zane gave me a small glare.

"Who'll choose you?" Lucky had a big bright smile on her face as she walked down the stairs in a simple white dress.

"These two fools think that you would actually give them a chance if I wasn't in the picture." Zane walked over to her and grabbed her hand. I smiled to myself as I watched him pull her into the crook of his arms. It was amazing to see Zane so protective and caring with Lucky.

"Oh, Leo. You're here." Lucky pulled away from Zane and ran up to Leo with a delighted face. "I didn't know you were coming over."

"Zane texted and said pizza was on the way." He laughed. "I couldn't say no to that, plus I haven't seen Noah since he's been back. I wanted to lay my eyes on him." He hugged her back tightly, and gave her a big kiss on the cheek. "You're looking positively radiant, Lucky. Probably the most beautiful mother-to-be I've ever seen. You almost make me want kids."

"You'll have gorgeous kids." Lucky blushed and grinned and I laughed at the murderous look on Zane's face as he watched her with his friend.

"It's a pity Zane got to you before me."

"That's enough, Leo." Zane walked over and stood next to Lucky. "Maybe it's time to get your own girl."

"No thanks." Leo shuddered. "I don't have time for the stress and drama that comes along with relationships – no offense, Lucky."

"None taken." She laughed and put her arms around Zane's waist. "Trust me, sometimes I wonder how I put up with this guy."

"Because you love me, duh."

"I won't love you so much if you keep embarrassing me."

"Sure." Zane laughed and walked into the kitchen. "You guys want a beer while we wait on the pizza?"

"I'll take a Bud." Leo lounged down on the chair and stared at me. "So, you dating anyone?" He gave me a quick look and I shook my head.

"Nah, not really. Not now that I have a kid to look after."

"A kid?" His eyes bulged wide open and I laughed.

"I adopted a little girl." I smiled. "You'll have to meet her."

"Whoa, I go away for a few weeks and I miss everything." Leo shook his head in wonderment and I was about to tell him more about Skylar when the doorbell rang. My heart thudded as I walked over to it quickly, hoping to see Robin on the other side.

"Hey," I opened the door with a wide smile and sighed when I saw the pizza deliveryman.

"Hey, pizza delivery." He said in a monotone voice. I tried not to roll my eyes at him or say something smart like "I thought you were the paperboy."

"What's the damage?" I took out my wallet and pulled out some bills.

"There is no damage to your pizza, Sir." The pimply-faced teenager looked at me with a blank expression.

"What?" I frowned and then realized he had misunderstood my question. "What's the total?"

"I didn't total anything, Sir. I only tapped the back of that car. It wasn't totaled at all." He stammered as he held the boxes in his hands, and it was at this point that I realized that he was either high or the biggest idiot I had ever met.

"How much money do I owe you?"

"You don't owe me, oh wait." He paused as he realized what I was asking. "A hundred should do it."

"A hundred dollars?" I asked him incredulously.

"Yes, Sir." He beamed at me and nodded. "A hundred dollars will take care of the bill nicely. Plus tip of course."

I grabbed the boxes from his hand and handed him $40, before glaring at him. "You better believe I'm going to call your boss and report you. Now get out of here. And don't try to pull this scam on anyone else."

"But Sir," his eyes widened in panic. "The bill is $55."

"Then I suggest you find $15 from somewhere." I smirked at him and slammed the door shut before he could say anything else. I turned around and saw that Lucky was standing right behind me, with a surprised expression, but laughter in her eyes. "Did that just happen?" I asked her and she burst out laughing.

"That was hilarious." She grinned, while wiping tears away. "If I hadn't just witnessed that, I would never have believed it."

"They're letting any old fool be a pizza delivery guy these days."

"What is the world coming to?" She grinned and shook her head. And then the doorbell rang again and she smiled at me. "You go and take those boxes to the kitchen and I'll take care of him this time."

"Okay," I grinned and walked back to the kitchen, sad that I wasn't going to get to hear Lucky give Dopey a piece of her mind. I put the boxes on the counter and pulled out some plates, while Zane opened up the bottles of beer.

"Shit, that pizza smells good." Zane groaned and opened up a box. "It tastes good too," he mumbled through a mouthful of pepperoni.

"Thanks for waiting on us all to get a plate before you started, greedy bear."

"Whatever." He laughed and handed me a beer. I took a swig of Bud and then froze as I heard a tinkle of feminine laughter that didn't belong to Lucky. Robin was here. I quickly placed the bottle back down and ran my hands through my hair. My heart started beating rapidly, and I turned around slowly before walking back into the living room with a big smile on my face. Joy poured through me when my eyes fell upon her – she looked as beautiful as I remembered her, and she looked happy as she stood there laughing. I stared at her for a moment, just memorizing her features, when a feeling of jealousy spread through me. Robin wasn't just laughing at some random joke. She was laughing up at Leo, who was laughing down at her, and very obviously admiring her goods. I felt a surge of anger as I stared at handsome Leo flirting with her. He was a blond Adonis and I knew that to most women, he was one of the most handsome and charismatic men they had ever met. I was scared that now that Robin had seen him, she wouldn't be interested in me; especially as we had already had a bit of a rocky start. I stood

20

there for a moment more just glaring at Leo, and then I caught myself. I was being just like Zane, only I didn't yet have the girl.

"Hi, Robin," I gave her a wide smile, trying to mask my jealousy, and she turned to look at me in what seemed like slow motion.

"Hi, Noah." She gave me a light smile and my heart flipped as our eyes met. All of a sudden, the room seemed empty. There was no one else in this moment than her and I, and every fiber of my body was aware of that fact. I walked over to her slowly, and she moved towards me as well until we stopped in front of each other and just stood there in front of each other, smiling like idiots.

"I'm starving." Leo's voice interrupted our moment and I looked up and saw a tinge of disappointment in his eyes.

"Me too." Robin turned towards him and smiled and his eyes lit up again. I frowned as they exchanged a small look. What was going on here?

"You always did love pizza." Leo laughed and I froze.

"You guys know each other?" I looked back and forth at them and noticed that Robin was blushing.

"Kinda." She mumbled and Leo nodded.

"We went on a few dates." Leo shrugged as he looked at me and I looked back at Robin.

"And then he just never called me again." She laughed, but I could tell that she was still hurt. "I guess that's what happens when you don't put out right away."

"That wasn't why I didn't call." Leo's voice was soft. "That wasn't why at all."

"Oh well, let's eat before the pizza gets cold." Lucky looked at Zane with a worried expression and ushered us all into the kitchen. "We can all catch up later after we eat."

"Hungry, are we Lucky?" Zane raised an eyebrow at her suggestively and she hit him in the arm.

"Yes, but not for you."

"That's hurtful." He pouted. "You better not try and jump on me tonight, I have a feeling I will be too tired."

"You're never too tired."

"Tonight I will be."

"Children, children." Robin grinned and walked past me and quickly into the kitchen behind them. I stood there for a moment and tried to control my breathing. Leo came and stood next to me and gave me a look.

"I didn't know you were dating Robin."

"I didn't know you dated Robin." I gave him a side look and his eyes looked pained.

"I didn't dump her because she wouldn't sleep with me." He sighed. "I really like her."

"Like or liked?" I frowned at his words.

"I don't know." He shook his head. "I didn't expect to see her tonight."

"I like her a lot." I bit my lower lip. "I can see her in my life forever."

"So could I." Leo looked away from me and mumbled under his breath.

"That was the problem." I pretended that I didn't hear him and looked away quickly.

"Well, it's good that you're a confirmed bachelor or this could have been a problem." I faked a laugh and gave him one quick glance before I walked into the kitchen. He was just standing there, and my stomach flipped with worry. Leo looked like anything but a confirmed bachelor at that moment and I had a feeling that my attempt to win Robin over was about to get a lot more complicated.

Chapter 3

Lucky

I was dreading going in to look at wedding dresses. I wasn't sure what size to get, since I wasn't sure how quickly I was going to grow. I also didn't know what color dress to get. Could I get a white dress if I was showing up at the altar with a big belly full of babies? The fact that I was a pregnant bride took away from the whole virginal maiden concept, and I didn't want to be a hypocrite. I was certainly no virgin.

"Whatcha doing?" Zane slid down on the couch next to me and picked up one of the magazines from the coffee table.

"Deciding what to wear to the wedding." I made a face at him and showed him the magazine in my hand. "I can't decide if I should dress traditionally or if I should get a short red dress, with a high slit and lace over the breasts."

"Hmm, do I get to decide?" Zane's hand slid around my waist and I giggled as I pushed him off.

"No, you don't."

"Is this going to be a striptease-type wedding?" His eyes sparkled at me. "Because if it is, I'd rather no one else be there but us."

"Uh huh." I rolled my eyes at him and his fingers slid up my torso again. "If you want we can practice the stripping part right now." His fingers crept across my right breast and paused. "You can start with your top if you want."

"I don't want."

"Aw, you're no fun, Lucky."

"All you think about is sex." I hit his fingers and shook my head. "I'm sure you'd love a striptease wedding. Maybe you'd like the wedding to be in the bedroom and officiated online. Maybe we can even be naked. That way you don't have to wait for the dress to come off."

"Uh oh." Zane pulled away from me and made a face. "What did I do now? Is this your PMS talking?"

"I'm pregnant, Zane. I'm not getting a period any time soon." I jumped up and threw the magazine on the couch. "And if you knew anything you would know that, you insensitive jerk. All you care about is sex."

"Oh God." Zane jumped up and made a face. "Are we going to have this conversation again?" He reached over and grabbed me, and grabbed my chin until I was looking up at him. "Do you really think I only want sex?" His blue eyes pierced into my soul as he stared at me tenderly and I could feel my heart melting as my anger dissipated. "Because you'd be right." He laughed at me, his eyes crinkling and I shook my head at him as I joined him in his laughter.

"You're lucky I don't take you seriously, Mr. Beaumont."

"What fun would that be, Mrs. Beaumont-to-be?"

"You can't say such things to a pregnant woman. We are emotional beings, you know."

"Really? I couldn't tell." He bent down and kissed me before pulling away. "Now how can I help you with your dress? Do you want me to come with you to try on dresses?"

"You can't see me in my wedding dress before we get married." I shook my head.

"Why not?"

"It's not allowed."

"Says who?"

"Says tradition. It's bad luck for the groom to see me in my wedding dress before the wedding."

"I've already seen your birthday suit, what does some dress matter?" He laughed.

"That's not the point." I groaned. "Everyone will know you've seen my birthday suit already, because I'll be fat at my wedding."

"You won't be fat."

"I'm going to look like a bloated pig. People are going to say it was a shotgun wedding." I sighed.

"It doesn't matter what people say."

"Yeah, to you. You're not the one that the priest is going to look at disapprovingly because you had sex before marriage."

"At least you're getting married and not going to raise them alone." Zane shrugged.

"Most women don't choose to be single mothers." I pushed him away from me. "That's the sort of attitude I'm talking about. You men have it so easy. You choose whether …."

"Lucky, I love you, but do we have to have another male-bashing conversation right now?" Zane pouted at me and I glared at him as he made faces at me trying to make me laugh.

"You think you can make everything better with a goofy face?"

"No, I think I can make everything better with sex. But I'm trying goofy faces first." He winked at me and I pursed my lips to stop myself from smiling at him. "I can see you're trying not to smile, Lucky."

"I'm going into the kitchen." I turned away from him with a huff and he followed me.

"We can always elope to Vegas, you know."

"That's not romantic." I sighed.

"We could make it romantic."

"I don't want to get married in Vegas. I want a proper wedding with a priest in a church, and I want my dad to give me away and I want my mom to help me." My lower lip trembled as I voiced the real reason for my sadness and anger.

"I'm sorry." Zane's voice was low and he looked at me sadly. "I know you miss them."

"Now more than ever." I looked at him with misty eyes. "Who's going to give me away?"

"I don't know." Zane looked at me with a worried expression. "I could."

"Zane, you cannot give me away." I giggled, slightly exasperated. "You're the one marrying me. You can't give yourself your blessing."

"I can if I want to." He smiled at me sweetly. "We don't have to have a traditional wedding, you know. You don't have to have someone give you away. You can walk up the aisle yourself. Or maybe we could have a beach wedding."

"A beach wedding would be nice." I smiled at him. "I was actually thinking about that."

"And maybe Noah could walk with you down the aisle."

"But isn't he your best man?"

"I think he can do both jobs." Zane smiled. "I'm sure he'd be happy to do both."

"Do you think so?" I asked hopefully, and then my heart sank. "I don't know if that would be fair, though. After everything that's going on with Robin."

"Don't remind me of that." Zane frowned. "What a mess."

"I know. I thought a fight was going to break out at the end of the night when Leo offered Robin a ride home."

"I know." Zane shook his head. "I've never seen Noah look so mad before."

"Poor Robin." I made a face. "What a position to be in."

"More like poor me. What a position for me to be in." Zane's eyes were wide. "My best friend and my brother are in love with the same girl."

"And from the looks of it, she has feelings for both." I continued. "Poor girl."

"Poor Noah."

"Poor Leo." I made a face. "One of them is going to be heartbroken." I chewed on my lower lip. "Though, I suppose I do have a replacement for one of them."

"If you mention Leeza's name, the wedding is off." Zane glared at me.

"Well, I guess I'm going to be a single mom then." I stared at him and he pulled me towards him.

"There is no way in hell you will ever be a single mom. I will be by your side forever. Even when you don't want me there." He growled before he kissed me hard, his lips pressing down on mine eagerly before he stuck his tongue into my mouth. "You are mine forever, Lucky Beaumont."

"I'm still Lucky Morgan right now."

"You're mine, no matter your name." He pulled away from me slightly and stared into my eyes. "You know that, right? We're a team. You never have to go through anything alone. No thought is too small or too petty to share with me. I want you to come to me with everything. I want to be here for you in every way."

"You're too sweet. What happened to the man I met in the diner?"

"I'm still here. I'm just a ball of mush now."

"I love you." I kissed his lips lightly. "Thank you for being you."

"No, thank you for marrying me."

"Thank you for asking."

"Thank you for having my babies."

"Thank you for loving our babies."

"Thank you for letting me have unprotected sex with you." He whispered and I hit him in the shoulder.

"Zane! Just when I think you're not going to be a dumbass."

"You wouldn't want me if I didn't entertain you."

"Whatever."

"What to go and have some unprotected sex?"

"What?" I glared at him.

"It's not like you can get pregnant right now."

"I swear you're lucky I love you, Zane Beaumont." I shook my head. "No, we are not going to have sex now. But yes, you can take me to the mall so that we can look at baby furniture."

"Oh no." He groaned. "Do I have to?"

"Do you want to attend a baby class with me tonight instead?"

"This is a trick question, isn't it?" He paused and narrowed his eyes. "You expect me to attend the class with you whether I like it or not, don't you?" He cocked his head to the side and a smile spread across his face. "Why Lucky, I do believe you're becoming a sly one, aren't you?"

"I have no idea what you're talking about." I laughed.

"Do we really have to go and look at cribs?"

"No," I paused and smiled slowly. "We can go and check out the diapers instead."

Zane groaned and put his face in his hands. "Diapers, cribs, baby classes. What have I done?"

"Tell me about it. I have to take next semester off."

"What?" He looked up at me. "Why?"

"I'll have a new baby. I can't handle school and motherhood."

"I'll be here to help."

"The man who doesn't know anything about babies?" I raised an eyebrow at him.

"I guess I can attend a few more classes with you."

"With no sexual innuendos?"

"You're really trying to take all the fun out of it, aren't you?"

"Fun is what got us in this position."

"Oh my God, we're going to be parents." Zane's face went pale and I knew that it was hitting him fresh all over again.

"We'll be fine."

"I'm glad one of us believes that."

"Let's have some fun tonight." An idea flashed into my mind. "Let's go to karaoke and just relax."

"I thought you wanted to go and look at baby stuff?"

"That can wait." I shook my head. "The stores will still be there tomorrow. Tonight I want us to go karaoke."

"Did I hear someone say karaoke?" Noah walked into the room with Skylar, who was sucking on a lollipop.

"What's ka-aoke?" Skylar looked at Noah with inquisitive eyes and bright blue lips. I tried not to laugh at the sight the two of them made. Noah was also sucking on a lollipop and he had bright green lips.

"It's when people go out and sing to well-known songs."

"Or not as well-known." Zane corrected him. "I remember you singing a certain song called 'Snakes going to get hurt' and no-one in the bar knew it."

"It was famous in France." Noah laughed and Skylar's eyes lit up.

"I wanna go to France and sing about snakes."

"Hmm, I'd rather you sing about cows and pigs on a farm." Noah smiled at her gently and ignored the other part of her comment. "In France?" she continued.

"No, we're not going to France." He tried to sigh, and I felt sorry for him and the memories the thought of France must be bringing up.

"We can play karaoke this weekend if you want, Skylar." I changed the subject and went over to the little girl. Her hair hung in soft blond tresses down her back and her big sky-blue eyes looked back at me hopefully. "We can sing all the songs you want to sing. We'll make it a party. You, me, Noah, Uncle Zane."

"And Aunty Robin and Uncle Leo?" she asked excitedly and starting jumping up and down.

"Stop." Noah's voice was a bit harsh. "Stop jumping, Skylar. You can hurt yourself jumping up and down with a lollipop in your mouth."

"Sorry, Noah." Her lower lip trembled and he bent down and hugged her.

"I didn't mean to raise my voice, Sky, I just want to make sure you don't harm yourself."

"Because you love me." She nodded as she spoke. "You only got a little mad because you love me and you want me to be okay. You would never harm me."

"Exactly, my love." Noah whispered into her ear and my heart melted as I watched the two of them. Then I thought about Zane being as loving with our children and tears came to my eyes. Zane and Noah were both so loving for two men who had grown up without the love of their parents. It made my heart ache and expand for both of them.

"I can't wait for my party." Skylar grinned and stared at me. "Maybe Uncle Leo will sing with me."

"Maybe." I smiled back at her, laughing inside. Skylar had barely met Leo for ten minutes when she had woken up and come downstairs the previous evening. But he had already won her over; something that Noah was none too pleased about.

"Leo may not be able to make it, Honey." Noah started and Skylar pouted. "But we'll see."

"Okay. I'm going to watch TV." Skylar ran into the living room and Noah stood up slowly.

"I guess the karaoke tonight is a private event?"

"Do you have a babysitter for Skylar?" Zane asked him pointedly and he grinned back at us, slightly embarrassed.

"Okay, okay. I forgot that part."

"Did you and Skylar have fun at the mall?" I asked and looked at the assortment of bags in his hands. "It looks like you were able to pick up a lot of goodies."

"She has clothes and toys for years now." His eyes grew wide. "For years, I tell you."

"More like a few months." I laughed, pleased that it had gone well. "Maybe I need you to help me choose a wedding dress."

"That's not fair." Zane interrupted. "How can he get to help and I can't?"

"Because he's not the one I'm marrying, unless you'd rather I change my mind and marry him. That way, you can help me pick a dress."

"Funny. Not." Zane put his arm around my waist. "If you keep making these jokes, I'm going to think you're serious."

"Who said they're jokes?" I stared at him with a deadpan face and then burst out laughing. "Don't be an idiot, Zane."

"I'm an idiot for your love."

"You mean a fool?"

"Huh?" He looked at me blankly.

"It's a song." Noah winked at me. "You may well be with the wrong brother, Lucky."

"Shut up, Noah." Zane growled and placed his lips on mine. He kissed me softly and his tongue traced along my lips, caressing me as his teeth nibbled. I melted against him and let out a sigh, before he pulled back with a satisfied grin. "And that's why you love me."

"Okay, guys. Get a room." Noah groaned and I looked up and saw a glimpse of envy in his eyes.

"How's Robin?" I asked him softly and he shook his head.

"No idea, haven't seen her since Leo took her home the other night." He shrugged, but I could hear the frustration in his voice.

"You should give her a call."

"If she wants to talk, she can call me." He made a face. "Or maybe she's fallen for Leo's blond good looks again and forgotten about me."

"Noah." I bit my lip. "Don't jump to conclusions. You don't know what's going on with her."

"She never told me she dated anyone. She made me feel like her last boyfriend was before she moved to Los Angeles."

"I don't think she considers Leo an ex."

"She obviously liked him." He frowned. "And he liked her."

"Well, he let her go." I touched his shoulder. "You know I love Leo, but he left her. He's old news."

"Yeah, but am I a better bet? I lied to her." His eyes looked pained as he looked back at me. "But, I have other things to worry about now. I'm going to go and watch TV with Skylar."

"Okay." I gave him a sympathetic look and then turned to Zane. "What are we going to do?"

"Nothing." He looked at me seriously. "This is none of our business. We're not going to do anything."

"But—."

"But nothing, we're not going to get involved with this." His eyes issued me a warning. "Robin needs to make her own decision."

"Fine." I looked up at him and kissed him on the lips. "I suppose that this once, you may be right."

"Has the world ended? Did you finally admit that I'm actually right about something?"

"Don't get used to it." I laughed and placed my head on his chest. "I do love you, Zane Beaumont."

"I know." He kissed the top of my head. "I love you too."

⌾

"I'm tired." Zane rubbed his eyes as we made it to the Mommy and Me store in the morning. "Couldn't we have made it to a later class?"

"Nope." I laughed. "It's not my fault you wanted to karaoke last night to every song you've ever heard before."

"I didn't want anyone to miss out on hearing my talent." He laughed and then groaned as he rubbed his head. "I think the gin and tonics helped."

"You did pack away quite a few." I grabbed his hand and guided him through the store as I looked for the instruction room.

"Well, when you told me you would drive I figured I might as well. But I guess I'm getting too old to be a party man."

"Yeah," I laughed. "You're my old man. You know what they say, mid-twenties is the new fifties."

"Very funny." He groaned again and squeezed my hand hard.

"Hi, are you guys here for Mommy and Me 101?" A cheerful man asked as we stopped at the door to a large room.

"Yes, we are." I smiled back at him and tried to ignore the weird look on Zane's face. I know he was wondering why a man was greeting us (in fact, so was I), but I decided to keep it in. I mean, so what if a man was

30

teaching the class, wasn't it sexist of me to assume that it should be a woman at the front?

"Have a seat. We'll be starting as soon as everyone gets here."

"What the fuck?" Zane whispered to me as we found seats towards the back of the class. "Is this a joke?"

"Don't be a male chauvinist." I sighed. "I'm sure he knows what he's doing."

"Excuse my language, but don't you find it a bit crazy that a man is teaching the Mommy and Me class? Like, is he going to be talking about vaginas? Won't that be weird?"

"Zane!" I blushed as I admonished him. "Be quiet."

"Okay." He rolled his eyes. "You let me know how it feels for a man to tell you what childbirth is like."

"He's just going to give us advice on what products we will need as new parents."

"Uh huh." He sat back and rolled his eyes. I pulled my seat away from him slightly and smiled widely at the new couple that walked into the room that looked as clueless as I felt.

"Is this the Mommy and Me class?" the girl asked, slightly timid, and the man gave her a huge grin.

"Yes, Ma'am. Have a seat." The couple exchanged a look and walked back towards us uncertainly.

"Even they think this is shady," Zane whispered to me. I ignored him.

"Hi," I smiled at the girl and she smiled back at me wordlessly. "I'm Lucky, and this is my fiancé Zane."

"I'm Diana and this is my boyfriend Gilbert." The guy, who looked slightly dopey, stared at us and nodded. "And yes, it is a bit ironic that I am Diana and he is Gilbert." She giggled. "People think I should change my name to Anne."

"Oh, okay." I smiled weakly, not sure what she was talking about.

"Diana even wanted to move to Prince Edward Island." Gilbert finally spoke up. "But I convinced her that would be too much."

"Uh, sure."

"Gilbert wants us to call our house 'The Gables' but I think that's too grand a name for a one-bedroom condo in Silver Lake." Diana continued and I could see Zane holding back a grin from the side of my eyes.

"So, are you guys having a baby?" I decided to change the subject.

"Not yet." Diana whispered. "But don't tell anyone. I don't want to get kicked out of the class."

31

"You guys decided to come to the class and you're not pregnant?" Zane finally spoke up and gave them a look.

"Gilbert and I are extreme couponers, like on the TV show." Diana said excitedly, her reserve fading. "We want to get a head start on the items we're going to need when we finally do have babies."

"It's never too early." Gilbert nodded.

"Well, I guess that's true." Zane gave me a look as if to say, 'these are your people,' and I gave him a quick glare.

"Can we sit next to you?" Diana said eagerly as she plopped herself down next to me. "If you want some help couponing I can tell you how to start. We have so much stuff, it's awesome. We just got a garden shed for $100, and it was originally $500."

"I thought you said you lived in a one-bedroom condo?" Zane asked, puzzled.

"Oh we do." Gilbert sat next to Zane and continued. "We had to get a storage facility to put it in, but it's a great investment for the future, when we are able to buy a house."

"How much is the storage facility?" Zane frowned.

"It's only $50 a month." Gilbert nodded eagerly. "We got a deal. It's meant to be $150 a month, but we signed a contract for 5 years, so now we get it for $50 a month."

"I see." Zane gave me another look and I turned to Diana, hoping that the next words out of her mouth weren't going to be too crazy.

"So have you and Gilbert been together long, then?" I smiled as her eyes widened with happiness.

"We've been together for six weeks." She nodded happily. "We met online and we knew right away, we were meant to be. We bought our place a month ago and now we're planning the rest of our lives together."

"You bought a house together a month ago?" I frowned. "After you were together two weeks?"

"When it's love, it's love." She giggled. "But we knew we had to. Gilbert found a great foreclosure deal so we decided to jump on it."

"I see."

"What about you and your fiancé?" She nodded at Zane, and then reached over and pinched me hard. "Good job, by the way. He's a hottie." She mouthed the words as if she were whispering, but her voice was so loud that everyone heard her.

32

"Thanks." I plastered a smile on my face and sat back and faced the front of the room. I could hear Zane laughing before he whispered in my ear.

"Bet you wish you had listened to your hottie fiancé right about now."

"Whatever." I turned to look at him, but gave him a brief smile when I saw his twinkling eyes.

"Okay, everyone. I guess we're going to get started." The man slammed the door closed and stood at the front of the class. "I guess everyone else got stuck in traffic. Their loss." His voice was aggressive and he looked pissed, as he messed around with some papers on his desk and mumbled something under his breath. "Anyways," he looked back up and made eye contact with all four of us. "My name is Mr. Joseph Markener. My rep number is 1w45y78a." He rushed the last part and I looked at him in confusion. "I have to give that last part for legal reasons," he flashed a fake smile. "But anyways, we can start." There was a knock at the door and his eyes lit up as he ran to open it up.

"Hello," he uttered eagerly, but his face fell as he saw a little boy.

"Is this the men's room?" the little boy asked curiously, and Joseph slammed the door in his face instead of replying.

"Stupid kid." He muttered under his breath and then turned back to us. "Okay, I want to ask a question of everyone first. How much money do you expect to spend on purchases before your baby is born? Let's go in a line, so everyone can answer." He nodded at Gilbert, "You can start."

"I expect to spend around $100 after all the coupons." Gilbert looked pleased with himself and Joseph glared at him.

"You," he nodded at Zane.

"I have no idea." Zane shrugged. "As much as it costs, I suppose."

"Oh, really?" Joseph's face lit up and he smiled widely at Zane. "Do you happen to have a Mommy and Me credit card?"

"No." Zane looked at him in confusion. "Why?"

"Oh, nothing." Joseph's eyes looked delighted. "But let's make sure to get you signed up before you leave. You'll get a 10% discount on your first order and I will make $100."

"Uh, I don't—" Zane started but Gilbert jumped in eagerly.

"Sign me up too. I love saving money."

"Of course, Sir." Joseph's frown was definitely gone now and he was smiling widely. "Okay, you." He pointed at me.

"I don't know exactly," I started. "But I'm thinking about $1,000."

"$1,000." Joseph laughed. "That's the cost of a good stroller."

"I don't think that—"

"Don't worry, young lady, I'll get you and your man sorted out." He grinned at me. "I know all the good products."

"I thought this class was going to be telling us what we should be thinking about buying and getting us ready for when we have our baby." I frowned. "I thought we were going to learn about bottling and bathing and how to choose a car seat."

"Don't worry, I'll be able to sell you all of that." He nodded eagerly. "And what about you, Ma'am, how much are you spending today?" He looked at Diana, and I felt very annoyed and slightly uncertain about the direction the class was going in.

"Well, it will depend on my boyfriend Gilbert." Diana started. "We currently have $5,000 in our joint checking account, but we can't spend anything until we come to an agreement."

"$5,000 is a good start." Joseph was practically rubbing his hands in glee. "Okay, well let's start with a quick video."

"Okay," I nodded, relieved. Now for the practical part of the class. I sat back expecting to see a new parents video starting when all of a sudden I saw Joseph's face on the screen.

"Hi, I'm Jospeh Markener, the new California rep for Bugabooboo products in California. We sell the best products for rich kids, and you can show them off to all your friends. Thanks for coming to my class. Today, via this video, I will show you the products you need to buy, and then after the video is done you can place an order." Joseph paused the DVD and looked at us. "Any questions?" There was silence in the room and then he pressed play again. I turned to Zane, annoyed that he hadn't said anything, and he just shrugged and looked back at the screen, his eyes laughing at me.

"Hey guys, it's me Joseph again. Now I'm going to tell you which Bugabooboo products you need to buy before you leave today. No need to take out a pen, I have it all noted down for you. Don't forget to open a store card as well." The screen then went fuzzy and I waited for Joseph to turn it off or say something, but instead he was staring at it intently. Within twenty seconds, his image appeared again and he was surrounded by a bunch of florescent yellow products.

"Hey guys, can you see me?" He laughed on the screen. "I wanted to tell…"

"Excuse me." Gilbert raised his hand and cleared his throat. "I have a question."

"You want to purchase everything already?" Joseph's eyes lit up. "It will take me a minute or two to go around the store and get you everything."

34

"No," Gilbert looked panicked and jumped up. "I just wanted to know when the sales start."

"What sales?" Joseph looked confused.

"The reject or discount sales." Gilbert grinned. "And if you could get us an employee discount that would be great."

"Employee discount?" Joseph's mouth fell open. "I can't do that."

"Well, when are the sales? We never buy unless an item is discounted by at least 50%," Gilbert continued, looking very serious.

"Yeah. We don't either." Zane spoke up. "In fact, I don't buy unless it's 60% off. Me and my lady don't have money to waste."

"Zane," I looked at him with a frown as I tried to stop myself from laughing.

"What, Lucky? We don't want to go wasting Joseph's time, do we? Not when he has so many Bugapoop products to sell."

"Bugabooboo." Diana corrected and we both looked at her. "It's Bugabooboo, right Joseph?"

He looked at us with a gobsmacked expression, and I used that as an excuse to jump up and grab Zane's hand. "Come on, Honey, I think I need to go to the toilet. Sorry to leave, you guys, but we have to go."

"Wait," Diana called after me. "Let me get your number so we can go on play dates."

"Play dates?" I turned round to look at her. This time it was my expression that looked stunned.

"You know: you, me and your kids." She smiled. "It would be fun."

"Oh my God, I think I'm going to bust." Zane shouted suddenly. "Lucky, take me home right now, or I may just bust."

"What?"

"Just do it." He hissed and I grabbed his hand and we hurried to the front of the room.

"Are you sure you don't want to sign up for a store card?" Joseph gave us one last hopeful glance, and we shook our heads as we hurried out of the room and into the main store.

"You owe me. You know that, right?" Zane shook his head at me and we laughed as we ran through the aisles.

"What was that?" I looked at him with a dazed expression as we exited the store.

"You tell me, my dear. You tell me."

"I thought it was going to be a good class."

"Who told you that?"

"I saw some reviews on Yelp." I blushed. "I figured other expectant mothers wouldn't lie."

"Maybe the other expectant mothers were all Joseph." Zane made a face. "Trying to sell as many Bugapoopie products as possible."

"Oh my God." I laughed. "I thought he was going to make us all open our wallets so he could see how much cash we had. And then have us call our credit card companies to see how much credit we could get."

"He would have been laughing with greed if he knew I had a $50,000 limit on my American express." Zane laughed and I stared at him in surprise.

"I didn't know you had a $50,000 limit." I made a face. "My highest limit is $1,000 and it's on my Capital One card that I got as a freshman in college."

"I can put you down on my card as an authorized user." Zane grinned. "Just don't get too spend-happy."

"I don't want to be on your card." I shook my head. "I don't want to spend your money."

"It's our money."

"No, it's not."

"Lucky, we're about to be married. What's yours is mine and what's mine is yours."

"Zane, I have twenty-five thousand dollars in student loans, about $450 in the bank, an $800 balance on my credit card and an old car that's not worth more than a couple hundred dollars."

"So? I have five bank accounts. One account has 45 million dollars."

"What?" My eyes went wide. "Shh." I looked around quickly. "You're joking, right?"

"No." He laughed and shrugged. "That's what happens when you have a dad that's rich as Trump, but doesn't give a shit. He plies me with money."

"Just you?" I frowned thinking about Noah and Skylar. "What about Noah?"

"He didn't like that Noah was a goody-two-shoes." Zane sighed. "He said he wasn't going to give money to someone who would just give it away."

"That's horrible."

"Don't worry. I give it away as well." He laughed. "So it all works out in the end."

"Do you give any to Noah?"

"He doesn't want any." Zane shook his head. "Though, I'm an investor in his documentary. The only investor, in fact."

"I love you, Zane."

"Good." He stared at me and brushed the hair away from my face as he looked into my eyes. "I love you, too. More than you'll ever know. I love you so much that I will let you bring me to a racket of a baby class like this and not even get mad."

"You know this was the best laugh you've had all week." I stared up into his eyes and grinned. "Without me in your life, it would be a dull existence."

"It was a dull existence until you came along. You brought the sunshine into my days." He leaned down and kissed me. "You put the rainbows in the sky. You are my tomorrow that came early."

"Did you think of that all by yourself?" I kissed him back happily, feeling comforted in his arms.

"I wrote another poem for you." He grinned down at me. "A super romantic one."

"Oh?" I pulled away and looked at him. "Let me hear it then."

"Lucky's too sexy, too sexy. Lucky's so sexy that I want to take her home. I want to take her to my bed. And have my wicked way with her."

"That doesn't rhyme and it's not romantic."

"Oh, did I say it was romantic?" He growled and his fingers ran across my ass. "I meant it was a super sexy one."

"Zane." I laughed and brushed his hands away. "We're still in front of the store."

"So?" He laughed. "These ladies know better than anyone what we're up to. They had to get pregnant somehow."

"Let's go." I grabbed his hand and pulled him with me.

"Where are we going?"

"Wherever you want?" I gave him my most seductive look. "I'm going to give you a treat for being a good boy today."

"Hell yes." He picked me up and swung me around. "Oops, sorry. Am I acting too excited right now?"

"A bit." I giggled. "Now take me somewhere before I change my mind."

"Your wish is my command, my love."

"More like your own wish."

"You know me too well." He laughed boyishly as he opened the car door for me.

"Thank you." I smiled sweetly as I got into the car, but all I could think about was how sexy he looked with his happy blue eyes and golden hair shining in the sun. I stared at his biceps as he closed the door and I swallowed hard as I saw his muscles ripple. Zane was so sexy and he was mine, and I was excited to show him how happy I was to have him in my life forever. At the end of the day, the wedding didn't matter, the baby products didn't matter. As long as we had each other and some understanding of what to do and how to cope, we would be fine.

Chapter 4

Zane

"Where next?" I stared at Lucky expectantly, wondering where she was taking us.

"Nowhere else." She grinned back at me and I studied her face in confusion. Did she have pregnancy brain again? I paused before I spoke up again as I had a feeling that she didn't appreciate me making comments that referenced her brain in a derogatory fashion.

"Um, okay. Did we get our wires crossed?"

"What do you mean?"

"I thought we were going to go and have some nookie somewhere." I shrugged. "Maybe I misunderstood."

"No, you got it right."

"Uh, okay. So where are we going?"

"We're here." She smiled again.

"We are?" I looked around the empty parking lot and frowned. "You wanna do it on the concrete?" I raised an eyebrow at her. "I don't have a blanket or anything, you know. I don't know how comfortable that'll be."

"Not on the concrete." She rolled her eyes at me and looked around the car. "I want to do it in here."

"In here?" I looked around and then it dawned on me. "Oh! You want to do it in the car."

"If you want." She grinned back at me and I laughed.

"As if that's a question."

"It will be our first time in a car."

"Oh, actually, I've done it in a car before." I answered stupidly.

"No, Dumbass." She glared at me. "I don't mean it will be the first time either of us has had sex in a car. I mean it's the first time we'll have had sex in a car together."

"You've had sex in a car before?" Jealousy tore through me at her words, and I shifted away from her.

"Not telling." She smiled coyly and I glared at her while my stomach clenched at the thought of her with another man.

"Is that why you want to have sex now? To remind you of him?"

39

"Are you being serious right now?" Her eyes widened and she shook her head slowly, allowing her hair to fall in her face. Wisps of curls surrounded her and she looked like a naughty angel as she stared at me with a slight smile.

"You're trying to make me jealous." I growled and pulled her towards me.

"Don't tell me about all the sex you've had with other girls if you don't want to hear about my escapades."

"I didn't tell you anything." *Grr, pregnancy brain.*

"You just said this isn't the first time you've had sex in a car."

"I didn't mean to…" I sighed and stopped talking. "Have you or haven't you had sex in a car before?"

"*I* haven't." She pulled away from me slightly.

"Good." I crushed my lips down on hers and pushed my tongue into her mouth so that she could feel and taste me as I consumed her. I tried to pull her closer to me, but the gearstick got in the way.

"Ow." She pulled back slightly and rubbed her hip. "That hurt."

"Sorry." I sat back and reached her hand down to my pants. "I'm just a little excited here."

"I'd say a bit more than a little." She giggled as she squeezed my hardness. "Actually a lot more than a little, you tease." I reached my hand up her shirt and caressed her breasts through her bra. She leaned in closer to me and I pulled her shirt off so I could also take her bra off. "Now you have to sit in my lap."

"How am I supposed to do that?" Lucky stared at me with a flushed face, her bra half off, and I couldn't talk as I stared at her perky breasts.

"What are you looking at, Zane?" Her face was hot and pink.

"Your boobs have grown." I stared at them in amazement and reached over to touch them gently. "Can I touch?"

"What?" She giggled. "Are you really asking?"

I laughed and squeezed the roundness of her breasts and then caressed her nipples. She moaned as I touched her nipples and her eyes grew heavy with desire.

"Oh, don't stop." She whispered and I grinned. I guess there were some pluses to her being pregnant, and even more sensitive nipples were a great plus. I reached over and bent my head down so that my lips were the ones teasing her and she wriggled in her seat as my teeth nibbled on her nipples. She arched her back as I tugged and sucked on her nipples gently and then I froze and pulled back quickly.

"What's wrong?" She stared at me in disappointment and surprise.

40

"Our babies are going to suck your nipples." I talked slowly as the thought hit me fully. "Your boobs are going to be working boobs. They're going to have milk and stuff."

"So?"

"I don't know. I just feel a bit weird. What if milk comes out while I'm sucking?"

"Are you joking?" Lucky started giggling. "Zane, did any milk just come out?"

"No." I spoke slowly and licked my lips. "I don't think so."

"We're months away from milk coming, Zane." Lucky shook her head. "And actually, that kinda turns some guys on."

"That's sick." I shuddered, thinking about accidentally swallowing a gallon of Lucky's milk as we made love.

"You're an idiot." She laughed. "It's just natural. And if we continue making love up until the babies come, then you might get a taste."

"Hmm." I thought about that for a moment. I wasn't sure I was going to be able to keep my hands off Lucky for any amount of time, but it freaked me out that I might sample the milk and… "Oh shit," I spoke aloud as I interrupted my own thoughts. "Do you think the babies will see me as I enter you?"

"Huh?" Lucky looked at me weirdly. "What are you talking about?"

"When we make love, will they see my cock sliding in and out?" I tried to ignore the look of laughter that had entered Lucky's warm chocolate brown eyes as she stared back at me. "It's not funny, Lucky. This could be a serious issue."

"I don't think it's a problem, Zane."

"What did the doctor say?" I asked her brusquely.

"What did the doctor say about what?" She sighed.

"About us making love before you give birth. Can I dislodge them?"

"Zane, you're big, but you're not that big." Lucky started laughing. "I'm pretty sure that everything'll be fine. But no, I didn't ask the doctor if your cock will harm the babies if we keep having sex. And he didn't ask me how big you were, either."

"Well, if he asks you can tell him 8 inches."

"You mean 4?" Lucky laughed and I pulled her hair. "Okay, okay. If he asks I will tell him 7 inches."

"Fine." I leaned over and kissed her again. "I'm not sure of the width. Should we measure that so you can…"

"Zane, shut up." She kissed me back hard and I rubbed her back as she melted against me. I attempted to pick her up so that she could sit in my

41

lap, but there wasn't enough room for her to fit on my lap next to the steering wheel. I reached down to the side of my chair and pushed it back as far as it could go. Lucky tried to climb on top of me and this time she barely fit in as she straddled me. She leaned forward and brushed her breasts against my lips before reaching down to unzip me and pull my hardness out of my pants. She sat back slightly and was able to pull my hardness out. My member grew at the touch of her fingers against my skin and I groaned as she caressed the tip of my cock, squeezed the pre-cum out and then ran her fingers back down the length of me. I closed my eyes and Lucky attempted to bend down to give me a blow job. I felt her lips on me for one second before she cried out in pain.

"Ow, ow. Don't move. Please don't move." She cried out and I peered down to see that her hair was stuck in my zipper. "Shit." Her fingers tugged at my pants as she attempted to detangle her hair.

"Watch it." I flinched as her fingers brushed against my cock roughly. "I don't think that pinch was on purpose." Lucky's eyes flashed at me as she continued playing around with my zipper and her hair.

"Ow," I muttered as the zipper chafed against my skin. "Are you trying to make it so I can never have kids again?" Lucky glared at me as her fingers pinched my foreskin as she tried to work her hair out.

"Just hold still, will you?" Her voice was brusque and she fiddled around some more before finally detangling her hair and sitting back. She looked at me with a wry smile before sliding back over to her own seat.

"Sorry about that." She made a face and I nodded as I stuffed my battered member back into my pants gingerly. "Do you want to try again?"

"Maybe not right now." I shook my head and smiled at her weakly.

"Maybe now we can go home and think of ways to distract ourselves from this incident."

"I guess we can invite Robin over." Lucky started hopefully and I shook my head again.

"Noah needs to sort this out by himself. If we get involved, someone is going to blame us. I don't want us to get caught up in any drama."

"There is no drama."

"Trust me – if we get involved, there's going to be drama." I gave her a warning look. "And we have our own problems to deal with."

"What problems?" She frowned at me as she pulled on her top.

"Well, the wedding, getting ready for the babies, deciding what you're going to do about school."

"I didn't know you considered the wedding and our babies problems."
I closed my eyes and counted to ten. *It's pregnancy brain, it's pregnancy brain. Don't react.* I repeated over to myself a number of times before I reached over and grabbed her hand. "I love you, Lucky."
"Uh huh." She pursed her lips and then let out a small sigh. "Sorry, I think I just need to go home and sleep."
"Are you tired?" I asked, slightly worried that our attempt to have sex in the car had been too much for her.
"A little bit." She nodded. "Sorry, but I just want to go back to the house and relax. Maybe we can discuss everything else tomorrow.
"Okay." I nodded and gave her a long meaningful look. I stared at her face and at her body in wonder and my heart beat quickly as I realized how blessed I was to have her in my life.

⁂

"Okay, Skylar, we have to be quiet." I put my fingers to my mouth as the little girl in front of me giggled at the mess we were making in the kitchen. "We don't want to wake Aunty Lucky up."
"I know, Uncle Zane." She giggled again. "But you look so funny."
"What?" I made a stern face at her. "I could never look funny."
"You have flour all over your nose." She walked towards me and tried to reach up to brush it away for me. Her small little arms didn't reach, so I lifted her up so she could do the job.
"I got all the flour." She smiled as she finished wiping my nose off and smiled into my eyes. "You have big blue eyes, like me." She said earnestly and I nodded at her.
"Yes, I do."
"But Noah has green eyes." She looked at me, considering. "How come he has green eyes and you have blue eyes?"
"We just got different features from our parents." I smiled as I put her down.
"Do you look like your mom or your dad?" She played with the cake batter we had made, and added more chocolate chips.
"I'm not sure." I attempted another smile at her, but this time it didn't spread to my eyes.
"My mom was beautiful," she continued, not noticing the effect her question'd had on me. "My daddy used to tell me all the time. She was so beautiful that Cinderella was jealous of her."
"Well, I guess we know where you got your beauty from." I grabbed up the bag of Nestle Toll House Morsels before she could pour any more in the bowl, and I pulled out some muffin pans.

43

"Do you think I look like Noah?" She looked up at me with wide eyes. "Like Noah?" My heart stopped and I paused as I waited for her to continue. Please God, don't let her ask me the difficult questions. I do not want to mess this up.

"I know he's not my real dad, but sometimes people start to look like their loved ones. I saw it on TV."

"You did?" I knew I sounded like an idiot, but I had no idea what to say.

"Yeah, it was on Disney." She nodded eagerly. "There were a bunch of dogs that looked like their owners."

"Oh, you mean dogs." I nodded, suddenly understanding. "I heard that as well. That dogs start to look like their owners." I thought for a moment, and then continued. "I'm not sure that means you will end up looking like Noah, though, no matter how much you love each other. But there's nothing wrong with that. It won't affect how much you love each other. And trust me, you're lucky that you're not going to end up looking like Noah." I laughed, and Skylar giggled before taking my hand in hers.

"You're funny, Uncle Zane."

"Please tell me again when Lucky is up." I joked, but I wasn't sure that she understood.

"You're going to be a good dad."

"Do you think so?" I asked, touched by her words. She nodded at me with big, wide, happy eyes and squeezed my hand.

"If Noah wasn't my new daddy, I would have chosen you." Her words were simple and short, but her honesty and trust melted every last worry and concern I had about being a father. I could do this. I could be a good dad. I didn't have to worry. It was weird how the fear had crept in so slowly. I hadn't even told Lucky about the deep worries I had about having to love and look after two babies. I was scared she would judge me or think I was a bad person. And it wasn't as if I didn't want the babies, it was more that I was worried that my heart couldn't fit in two more people. I was worried that I couldn't love them as much as I loved Lucky. I was scared that I would fuck them up and ruin their lives, and that I would have no clue what I was doing. But Skylar had erased all of those fears with eleven words.

"You know I'm always here for you, Skylar." I reached down and hugged her close to me.

"Hey, hey, what's going on?" Noah sauntered into the room and his eyes widened as he surveyed the mess around us. "Did a bomb go off in here?"

"No, Noah," Skylar giggled and ran over to him. "We're making cookies for Lucky for when she wakes up."

"What about me?" Noah joked. "Don't I get any cookies as well?"

"You don't need cookies." She shook her head.

"Who've you been talking to?" He grinned and rubbed the top of her head. "I was going to offer to help you both tidy up if I was going to get some of the cookies, but I guess not."

"You can have some, you can have some." She squealed and I laughed as Noah picked her up and swung her around. "Put me down," she giggled. "I'm going to get dizzy."

"Are you going to let me have some cookies?"

"Yes, Noah," she laughed as he finally set her back down on the floor.

"You can start with the dishes if you want." I motioned to the sink, and Noah laughed and shook his head.

"I think not, Bro. How's about I finish the cookies, but on a baking sheet? You do know that cookies and cupcakes aren't the same thing, right?" He nodded towards the muffin trays and I shrugged as I chuckled.

"Fine, fine. I'll start the dishes."

"Where's Lucky?" he questioned as I turned on the faucets and started filling up the sink.

"She's resting. She was a bit tired after our trip today."

"Lots of shopping?"

"No, actually. No shopping." I rolled my eyes. "And no sex."

"Zane." Noah's eyes flashed at me as he nodded at Skylar, who was pulling out chocolate chips from the batter and eating them.

"Oops, sorry." I made a face. "But yeah, anyways. We didn't get much accomplished today."

"Did you guys pick a date for the wedding?" He looked at me curiously and I shook my head.

"Nah." I sighed. "I think it's stressing her out."

"That's not good."

"Yeah. I still think we should just elope to Vegas."

"I doubt she thinks that's romantic." Noah rolled his eyes. "Sometimes I really wonder about you, Bro."

"What's wrong with Vegas?"

"I'm not even going to go down this road with you." Noah added some more flour to the mixture in the bowl. "Did you add any baking soda to this?"

"Baking soda?"

45

"I guess that's a no." He laughed and went over to the cupboard. "When did you become the culinary king?"

"When I went into hiding." He laughed. "I can whip up all sorts of things now."

"Then please do. I'm getting fed up with your pizza delivery surprises," I joked, starting to wash up the dishes. "Hey, do you think I should tell Lucky we should wait to get married until after the babies come?" I asked seriously.

"Is that what she wants?"

"I don't know. I don't think so." I bit my lower lip and thought. "I think she wanted us to be legally married when the babies were born, but I know planning the wedding is stressing her out."

"So why don't you plan it?"

"Plan it?" I looked at him, aghast. "You're joking, right?"

"No. No, I'm not. Why can't you plan it? Maybe even make it a romantic surprise."

"How am I supposed to plan a wedding?" I shook my head and scrubbed the plates. "I have no idea what to do."

"I'm sure you know as much as she does. Just think how sweet and romantic that would be." Noah nodded to himself. "I think that Lucky would really appreciate you surprising her like that."

"Do you really think so?" I looked at him thoughtfully. "It might take a lot of pressure off her mind."

"Yes, do it." He laughed. "Trust me, you will win the fiancé of the year award."

"I need to win something like that. Or at least be entered into the contest." I gave him a wry grin. "Anyways, enough about me. How's it going with Robin?"

"Ugh, I don't want to talk about it." He made a face at me. "Let's just say I don't think Skylar will be calling her 'Mom' anytime soon."

"Oh, sorry." I patted him on the back. "What about your mom? How's it going with her?" I asked softly. Surprisingly, I held no ill will when I spoke about his mom anymore. Even in my mind, the bitterness and pain were no longer there. I think because I knew my real mom loved me, it didn't hurt me as much anymore.

"No idea." He shrugged and turned away. "Let's get these cookies in the oven and finish tidying up before Lucky wakes up and kills us all."

"That sounds like a plan," I said, laughing. I went back to washing the dishes and looked back to see Noah placing small gobs of the cookie dough on a baking sheet. I felt bad that he had no relationship with his mom; she was alive and well, and even though she was a bitch I knew she loved him. He had waited his whole life to find her, and now they had no relationship because of me. I knew in my heart that I had to do something to mend their relationship.

⚜

"These are delicious." Lucky licked the crumbs off of her lips and Skylar giggled as she munched on the freshly baked cookies.

"Me and Uncle Zane made them for you."

"Don't forget me," Noah piped up and I gave him a look.

"You can't let me have credit for anything, can you?" I joked and we both laughed.

"You guys are all spoiling me way too much." Lucky giggled. "I'm not going to want to do anything once the babies're born."

"Can I play with the babies once they're born?" Skylar looked at her hopefully.

"Yes, but we will have to be very careful." Lucky rubbed her hair and Skylar cuddled into her. "Babies are very delicate."

"Much like me." I grinned and she looked over at me and we shared a smile. Lucky looked beautiful and rosy as she smiled up at me with light and shining eyes. My heart expanded with love and I decided then and there that I was going to plan the wedding. It would all be a surprise.

"Let's play a game." Skylar looked over at me excitedly. "I wanna play Monopoly."

"You're not playing anything but bedtime, Young Lady." Noah shook his head and picked her up off the couch.

"But I'm not tired!" She moaned and squealed at the same time as he tickled her.

"You have things to do tomorrow." He started walking towards the stairs and then paused and looked back at Lucky and I. "I'm going to read Skylar a bedtime story and then I have to pop out for a bit. Do you guys mind watching her?"

"Not at all." Lucky smiled back at him and I held in a sigh. I didn't want to look after Skylar. I wanted to make sweet love to my fiancé, but I supposed I could wait until Noah got home. I certainly wasn't going to risk Skylar walking in on our lovemaking and screaming out in fright as Lucky and I moaned and groaned in ecstasy.

"Great, thanks." Noah smiled and turned and went up the stairs. "You guys rock."

"Yeah, I wish I had free, live-in babysitting services." I mumbled as he went up the stairs and Lucky walked over to me and kissed me on the cheek.

"What's the problem now, Grumpy?" She teased me and grabbed my hand and led me over to the couch.

"I'm not grumpy." I made a face at her as we sat down.

"Uh huh." She grinned and rubbed her fingers across my cheeks and lips.

"Did you sleep well?" I smiled at her. "No nightmares from earlier, right?"

"No nightmares. I had very sweet dreams." She slipped a finger into my mouth and I sucked on it as I stared back at her.

"Oh yeah? What did you dream?"

"I dreamt that we didn't have any complications in the car."

"Oh yeah?"

"Yeah." She removed her finger and replaced it with her tongue, allowing it to trace the lines of my lips before plunging into my mouth. "I dreamt that we had no problems at all."

"Was it everything that you imagined?" I breathed heavily as my pants suddenly felt tighter.

"Not really." She shook her head with wide eyes. "I hadn't imagined you bending me over the hood of the car like that."

"What?" I mouthed back, enraptured by her words.

"Yeah," She grinned back at me. "Sex in a car I'd imagined before. But sex in the parking lot, sprawled out on top of the car wasn't something I'd ever thought about."

"I've thought about it before." I laughed and captured her darting tongue with my lips. "I've pictured your tight little ass up high in the air as I've fucked you from behind as you gripped onto the metal and cried out my name begging for me to never stop."

"Really?" This time it was her breathing that was heavy and deep and she moved in closer to me. "You've never told me that before."

"I didn't want to scare you." My hand slid up from her waist and cupped her breast. "I didn't want you to think I was a sex fiend."

"But I already know you're a sex fiend." She gasped as my fingers pinched her nipple.

"But that's not all that I want." I whispered against her lips.

"I know."

"Though, sometimes I do think of pushing it further, taking it to the extreme."

"What's extreme?" She gasped, her pupils dilated as my other hand found its way to her other breast.

"I don't know." I shifted in the seat and she moved over quickly and straddled my lap. "What's extreme to me may not be extreme to you."

"Public sex isn't extreme." She smiled down as she gyrated on my lap.

"I guess it depends on how public."

"Not where anyone can see." She laughed and my hands played with her long hair.

"Isn't that part of the thrill? That someone might see?"

"I don't want anyone to see." Her eyes were wide and I slid my hands up under her top and caressed her waist.

"No one has to see." I shook my head. "I don't want anyone to see you either."

"Okay, good."

"I was thinking we should write our own vows." I burst out and she stopped in mid-gyration, her face looking puzzled.

"What?" She looked down at me, and I lifted her up and shifted her slightly so that she wasn't sitting directly on my hardness. I wasn't sure I would be able to resist fucking her on the couch if she remained in that position.

"Sorry, completely different thought, but I was thinking that maybe we can write our own vows. As opposed to just saying the words the church provides."

"Oh okay." She looked pleasantly surprised. "Sure, we can do that."

"Good." I kissed her nose. "And maybe we should stop with the public sex talk right now. I'm not sure I'm going to be able to stop myself from ripping off your clothes and taking you right here if we keep up."

"I don't mind." She started moving back and forth on my lap.

"You may not mind, but I'm not sure if Noah will be too happy to walk back downstairs and see us fucking in the living room."

"Oh yeah." She blushed red and moved off of my lap. "I forgot."

"You didn't have to move away completely. I kinda liked the feel of you on me." I tried to pull her back on top of me and she shook her head.

"Not right now."

"Then when?" I groaned, starting to feel a bit grumpy again.

"Tonight."

"Promise?" I asked hopefully.

"Yes, as soon as Noah comes back we can go to the bedroom, lock the door and have our wicked ways with each other."

49

"You promise to be wicked with me?" My eyes were alight with mischief, and she hit me in the shoulder as I started laughing.

"I'll be as wicked with you as you are with me."

"Then it promises to be a very wicked night." I winked at her and she gave me a slightly wary look. I looked at the clock and prayed that whatever Noah had to do would be done very quickly.

Chapter 5

Noah

I left the house feeling guilty. Zane and Lucky were on the couch looking like all they wanted to do was rip each other's clothes off, and I was the one stopping them from doing just that. I felt so guilty that I almost decided to stay home, but I knew that I had to go and see Robin. I needed to know where we stood. I was fed up with feeling unsure and jealous. And I was also worried that Leo was already making his move. He was Zane's best friend and also a friend of mine, but I knew that all was fair in love and war. If Robin had affected him as much as she had affected me, then I knew he would be trying to get her back.

I pulled into the parking lot and sat there for a few minutes thinking about what I wanted to say. I didn't really know what would be appropriate. It wasn't like I could express my undying love and wish to marry her. I wasn't really sure if that would ever happen for us, though I hoped that one day that it could. I liked Robin a lot, and she had really touched my life, but I didn't really know her. I wanted to know her better. I wanted to continue developing our relationship. But I didn't know if I had already ruined that opportunity.

I got out of the car slowly, walked to her apartment, and knocked on the door with my heart in my mouth. I could hear the television on as I waited and I wondered if she would be happy or mad to see me whenh she opened the door.

"Coming, I'm just getting my purse." I heard her call out and I realized she must think I was some delivery man. I smiled to myself at the thought of getting to eat some delicious food as we talked; I was slightly hungry.

"Hey, sorry about that." She opened the door, looking sexy and frazzled with a bunch of notes in her hand. "I was just getting the money." She looked up at me, and her expression looked shocked as she made eye contact with me. "Noah."

"Yes, it's me." I laughed. "Not the food. Though, I'll pay if you let me share it with you."

"I didn't know you were coming over." She bit her lower lip.

"Can I come in?" I smiled. "I promise I don't bite."

"I, uh, I kinda have company." Her face flushed and my heart stilled.
"Oh?" *Please don't let it be Leo.*
"I, uh," she stammered and paused as we both heard footsteps walking to the door. I looked around her body and into the apartment, and saw Leo standing there with a bottle of wine in his hands.
"I see." I nodded and gave her a sad look. "I guess I know where I stand."
"No." She shook her head and grabbed my hand. "It's not like that."
"Uh huh." I pulled my hand away from her and she stepped out the door.
"He just showed up as well, but about 10 minutes ago."
"I see." I looked at her with doubt in my eyes.
"It's true." Leo walked to the door and stared at me. "I guess we both had the same idea." I turned to look at him and he gave me a short smile, which I returned. I stared at the two of them standing there, and I knew that my next move was most probably the most important move I could make. If I left right now, I was possibly throwing them into each other's arms. It would be like accepting defeat.
"Well, if you don't mind, maybe I can come in as well." I squared my shoulders and gave Robin my most dazzling smile.
"I, uh," she stared into my eyes and gave me a half smile.
"Great." I grinned and walked into the door. "Good to see you, Leo. I hope you don't mind that I'm crashing the party as well."
"Yeah, I don't mind." He frowned at me and we all stood there awkwardly for a few moments.
"Wine, anyone?" Robin walked towards the kitchen quickly without looking at either of us, and Leo and I followed behind her.
"May the best man win," Leo gave me another short smile and I nodded.
"To the best man."

<hr />

"So Zane's going to plan the wedding?" Robin's eyes were wide with excitement as she stared at me. "That is so romantic."
"Yeah, it was my idea." I nodded, happy that I had all of her attention, even though she was sitting next to Leo on the couch. "I think it will really take the pressure off her."
"Wow, that's just an awesome idea."
"Really?" Leo frowned. "Not to be rude, but Zane knows shit about weddings. This is meant to be Lucky's one big day. She doesn't want a

picnic catered by McDonalds. That's not going to be the wedding of her dreams."

"Zane's not going to cater his wedding with McDonalds." I shot back at him.

"Oh yeah, better yet: Papa John's."

"Now, now, guys." Robin smiled at both of us gently. "I think it's a cute idea. I mean, there is a lot of potential for Zane to mess it up, but it's still a good idea."

"My brother won't mess it up. Plus, I'll help him."

"Because you know better?" Leo laughed. "That's the blind leading the blind."

"At least I've had a real relationship." I gave him a pointed look.

"Well, I'm not sure I want a real relationship if the girl turns out to be a drug dealer or willing to hand over her stepdaughter." Leo shot back, and there was silence in the room. Robin gave him a disappointed look, and I shook my head at his words. "Sorry," he sighed. "That wasn't called for."

"No, it wasn't." I bit my lower lip. "Though, I suppose it was true. I don't have the best track record." I shrugged. "I'm hoping that has changed now, though." I smiled at Robin and she gave me a shy smile in response. "I know I've messed up plenty of times, but I don't want to keep making those mistakes again."

"Okay, okay. I'm getting the hint." Leo shook his head and sighed. "I know when I'm not wanted." He stood up and gave me a wry smile. "You're a good guy, Noah. I know when I'm beaten."

"What?" I looked up at him in shock. *This was it?*

"I'm just leaving before I get kicked out." He laughed and looked at Robin with regret. "I had my chance and I messed up. I'm sorry." He gave her a meaningful glance and she smiled back at him.

"It's okay." She stood up and hugged him. "We were both in a bad place."

"Are you leaving?" I stood up as well, not wanting them to all of a sudden have some moment.

"I don't know that I was ever really wanted." He ran his hands through his hair and chuckled.

"Of course you were." Robin reassured him and then looked at me. "But just as a friend, you're right. I like Noah. I'm not sure what's going to happen, but right now I want to see how it goes."

"I appreciate your honesty." Leo sighed and my heart started racing. He gave her a sweet smile and leaned down to peck her on the lips. "If it doesn't work out with Noah, give me a call."

"Will do." She smiled.

"I wouldn't hold your breath." I winked at him and Leo laughed.

"You're a better man than me, Noah. I would have kicked your ass so far out the door that you would never've come back."

"Violence isn't the answer. At least not when the other guy is my brother's best friend."

"About that." Leo pulled out his phone. "Do let your brother know he can call me back now. The air has been cleared."

"Will do." I laughed and sat back on the couch as Robin escorted Leo to the front door. I wanted to go with them to make sure he didn't try to slip in another kiss, but knew I'd be pushing my luck if I started acting like a jealous boyfriend already. I waited for Robin to come back, impatiently. All I wanted to do was kiss her and hold her close.

"Hey," she walked into the room and looked at me almost shyly. "Well, that wasn't awkward at all."

"Hey, at least a fistfight didn't break out."

"True," she looked at me wickedly. "Though, it would have been quite exciting to have two men fighting over me."

"You want to see me with a black eye? You know that Leo has worked as a body guard."

"You've got some muscles on you there." She stared at my arms appreciatively.

"Well, I try." I jumped up and walked over to her. "I guess they could do some damage."

"I bet." She shivered and I couldn't help myself anymore. I reached over and pulled her towards me, looking into her eyes for her permission before I kissed her. She nodded slightly and that was all I needed before I pressed my lips down on hers. I felt a fever in my head as our lips met and a spark of heat flew down my spine. My body had missed her even more than I thought.

"You're cold." I grabbed her hands and rubbed them in mine.

"It's a cold night."

"Not really," I looked up at her in concern. "Are you sick?"

"No." She smiled. "Though I do feel feverish inside."

"Oh no." I raised my head to her forehead to see if she had a temperature.

"I think I need the doctor to tend to me."

"Oh really?"

"Yes, Doctor. I think you need to examine me."

"Hmm, I think I need you naked if I'm to do a proper examination."

"I may need help taking my clothes off."

"I can certainly oblige with removing clothes; in fact, it's a specialty of mine."

"Ooh, I like being with professionals." She giggled and I grabbed the buttons on her blouse and pulled her towards me.

"I like being with you as well."

"So what are you going to do to me, Doctor?"

"I'm going to make you all better." I growled in her ear and she moaned as I pulled her top off. I stared at her for a few moments in her lacy cream bra and then unclasped it and pulled it off. "First, I'm going to examine your breasts and make sure everything is okay."

"Oh, Doctor, that tickles."

"Really?" I paused. "Maybe I'm examining them incorrectly." I bent down and traced my tongue around her breast before taking her nipple into my mouth.

"Oh, Doctor." She let out a sigh as she rested her head back and ran her hands through my hair.

"The left breast seems fine." I grinned at her wickedly and then moved over to the right breast. "Now on to the next."

"You're going to make me feel like a pervert the next time I go in for a mammogram. You know that, right?"

"Just remember that your regular doctors shouldn't be checking you this way." I grinned up at her before nibbling on her right nipple. She cried out and I smiled. "Just testing that you still have sensitivity there."

"Ass." She laughed and I reached down to her pants.

"Are you ready for further testing, Robin?"

"Yes, Doctor." She grinned excitedly and I picked her up and carried her to the bedroom.

"I've missed you." I couldn't stop myself from uttering as I laid her down.

"I've missed you as well." She purred up at me.

"I mean, I've really missed you. I'm sorry, you know that, right? I didn't mean to keep anything from you. I just didn't want to…"

"Shh." She placed a finger on my lips. "Let's not talk about this now."

"I don't want you to think that this is just about sex for me. It means so much more than that to me."

"It means more to me as well." Her eyes pleaded with me to let it go. I decided to ignore the voice in my head that said to talk before we had sex. Sex wasn't going to absolve her fears. But I couldn't resist myself as she wiggled in the bed below me. I stared at her perky breasts as they jiggled and brushed against my chest. I couldn't resist her. I was attracted to her, like a moth to a flame, and right now neither of us was worried about getting burned. But that's what sexual attraction does to people. It makes you forget about all the other problems bubbling at the surface.

"I'm going to make love to you gently and slowly and then I'm going to…"

"No need to be gentle." She shook her head. "I've been a bad girl. Treat me like a bad girl."

"You want me to spank you?"

"I want you to make me forget my own name." Her eyes sparkled at me. "I'll fuck you so good that all you can think about is my name." I pushed her back on the bed and unbuckled her pants roughly. "And I won't let you come until you beg me."

"Oh, Noah." She closed her eyes and my fingers ran up her inner thigh and stopped at the edge of her panties. My finger traced an invisible line along the middle of her panties and she gasped as my finger roughly rubbed her bud.

"Touch me, Noah."

"Shh. I'm in charge." I looked down at her and covered her mouth with mine, enjoying the look of surprise in her eyes at my roughness.

"I need to feel you." She whispered and I removed my fingers from her panties. She groaned in frustration and I gave her a stern look.

"The doctor's in the house, and he's making the rules tonight."

"But I want to feel your cock in me so bad, Noah." Her voice sounded like it was singing. "I've been aching for your touch."

"Don't say that." I groaned. "You're going to make me come before I even take my pants off."

"No, I won't." She laughed.

"Trust me, you will." I caressed her cheek as I kissed her. "It hasn't been that long, but my body has been missing you."

"Not as much as I've been missing you."

"Even though you've been mad at me?"

"That hasn't stopped me from masturbating to thoughts of you every night."

"You think of me when you pleasure yourself?" A warm and happy feeling spread through me at her words.

"Every single time."

"I guess it shouldn't surprise you that I've been thinking of you as well."

"What do you think about?" She whispered in my ear and reached up to pull my shirt off. I knew that if I was staying in character I should tell her off, but I was too excited by the feel of her fingers against my skin.

"I think about you touching me and kissing me." I muttered gruffly as her fingers worked their way down my pants. "Only it never felt this good."

"Your dreams of me could never live up to the reality of me," she whispered softly in my ear.

"You're right about that." I closed my eyes and fell back on the bed, my aggressor role long gone.

"Make love to me, Noah." She curled up next to me. "I just want to feel you."

"You don't have to ask me twice." I pulled her on top of me and sank my teeth into her neck as my hand found its way back down her body.

<hr/>

"I'm going to have the best sleep." Robin purred next to me, after her third orgasm of the night. "I'm not sure that I'm ever going to have a good night's sleep without you in my bed."

"I'm glad that I'm able to satisfy you in more than one way." I smiled at her gently, but as I glanced at the clock on her bedside table I felt a sudden jolt of panic.

"What's wrong?" She gave me a small look of fear.

"Nothing's wrong." I sighed and sat up and looked down at her angelic face as she lay there naked next to me, with her hair flowing down her body. "But I think I have to go."

"Go?" She frowned and looked at me in disappointment. "You can't go, it's 3 a.m." She looked at the clock as well.

"I'm sorry, but I don't want to be missing when Skylar wakes up in the morning."

"Oh." She bit her lower lip and looked away from me. "Bye, then."

"I know it's shitty. I'm sorry." I got out of the bed and stood there looking at her, hoping she would look at me and understand how much I wanted to stay the night with her. "You know I had a wonderful night, right?"

"Sure, booty calls are normally wonderful."

"It wasn't a booty call, for me." I grabbed her hands and made her look at me. "Don't say that."

"It sure feels like a booty call. You got what you needed. Heck, the other guy even walked away before you even had to prove your worth. It's all so easy for you, isn't it, Noah Beaumont?"

"Don't be like this, Robin." I sat on the bed and looked at her with sorrowful eyes. "I really like you and I want to see where this can go. This isn't just about sex, but I can't stay the night. I have responsibilities now. I have a child. I have to be there for her when she wakes up in the morning. It wouldn't be fair to her if I wasn't there. She wouldn't understand why I'm not there in the morning." I repeated more firmly, willing her to understand.

"It's fine." Robin's eyes glazed over. "I understand. Just go."

"I'm not going to just go when you're in this mood."

"What do you want me to say, Noah?" She shrugged. "I get it. You have a kid now. A kid I didn't even know existed until she showed up."

"I'm sorry I didn't explain about her. It was hard for me to talk about my relationship with Monica and Skylar. I didn't want to scare you or make you think I was crazy. It was a strange situation to be in. I wasn't even sure what I was going to do. I had just met you. I didn't want to scare you away."

"You did a good thing, Noah." She sighed and grabbed my hands and smiled at me weakly. There were tears in her eyes and my heart froze. "Trust me, I wish that someone would have loved me enough to do whatever it took to make my life better."

"Your foster parents loved you."

"They did, but they had so many children." She sighed. "Sometimes, you just want to feel special."

"I can understand that."

"Like right now. I love what you've done for Skylar, Noah. I absolutely love it. You're such a great man for taking a child that isn't even yours. You're dedicated to her well-being already, and you want the best for her. You're thinking of her first in your life. She is your life right now."

"Yes, yes she is." I nodded, glad she understood where I was coming from.

"But," She paused and gave me a look that sent shivers down my spine. "I want to be first in the guy I date's life right now. I want to be number one, I want to be the one you want to make happy. I want you to stay with me because that's what you want, and because you know it will make me happy."

"You don't know how bad I want to stay," I started, but she shook her head and stopped me.

"But you can't. I can never be your number one." She lay back and closed her eyes. "I dare say I sound like a selfish bitch right now. But I've never been a first priority. I want it so bad. I want to be with you, Noah. I like you so much. But I need to know what it feels like to be number one. I want to be the most important person in someone's life. That's all I've ever wanted."

"I can't give you that right now," I mumbled as I felt my heart breaking.

"I know." Her voice sounded pained. "Maybe we should just forget this."

"Are you joking?" I pulled her up and made her look at me. "Are you fucking joking me, Robin?" Her eyes popped open in shock as she looked at me.

"What?"

"Don't be stupid here, Robin. I'm going to pretend that your words are coming from a place of hurt and upset. I understand your need to be number one in someone's life. And you would be the number one woman in my life. There is no one else I'd rather date right now. We have a special connection. Yes, I have a daughter. Yes, she is who I have to think about first. But we're adults, Robin. We've both been through shit, but we'd be fools to let what we have go because of something this stupid. I've already fucked up once, but I've been lucky. You've forgiven me and you're willing to give me a second chance. I'm not going to screw that up. But you're not going to hold Skylar against me. You're not that kind of woman. At least, the woman I'm falling in love with is not that woman. Don't tell me I got you wrong." I stopped and looked at her with my heart beating quickly. This was it. I'd laid it all on the line. This was make or break.

"You have more faith in me than I have in myself." She laughed lightly and sat up, so that she was staring into my eyes. "And you're willing to fight for me, for us." She sighed and a lone tear rolled down her face. "I'm fucked up, Noah. I don't know how to handle emotions. I'm scared that I'm going to get hurt."

"I will never hurt you, Robin. I promise."

"But that's not something you can really promise, is it?" She ran her hands through her hair. "You're such a good man. When I look at you, I almost forget that I'm me, carrying the problems of the world on my shoulders."

"I can help take care of that burden." I moved in closer to her so that she could see the sincerity in my eyes. "I want to take on some of that burden. And I want you to bond with Skylar, if you're willing to do that."

"Are you sure?" She looked at me with uncertain eyes.

"Yes, I want you to know that if this goes any further, it is a package deal. You met me as a single man, but now I'm a man with his daughter." I paused. "A man that would one day like to take a wife and provide a mother and more children to his daughter's life." Robin's eyes widened at my words and I smiled at her gently. "I hope I'm not scaring you. I'm not telling you that I need or want you to marry me and become Skylar's mom right away, but if things work out, that's the ultimate goal. If you don't think you could ever take on that role, I want you to tell me."

"I've always wanted my own family," she said slowly and my lips crushed down on hers as my heart exploded in happiness and hope. Maybe we really did have a chance at finding our forever love together.

Chapter 6

Lucky

"I cannot believe that Noah stayed out all night." Zane's voice was furious as we lay in bed. "He is seriously going to hear it from me."

"He didn't stay out all night, Hon. He came back early this morning."

"Creeping in at 5 a.m. is not acceptable." He glared at me as he played with the loose curls running down my back.

"Don't be irritable," I bent down and kissed him lightly. "There will be other nights to make love."

"When?" He frowned. "It seems like I might never get laid again."

"Zane!"

"What?" He shrugged. "It's true."

"We nearly made love last night."

"Yeah, but we didn't." He sat up and I laughed at his pouty expression. It amazed me how there were moments when I looked in his face and he looked like a petulant school boy even though he was my fiancé and the love of my life, and most definitely a man. "What's so funny?" He continued grumpily.

"Go back to sleep, Darling. I think you need some more rest." I laughed as I jumped out of bed and made my way to the bathroom.

"I need some ass, is what I need."

"I'm glad you love me for my brain." I rolled my eyes and yelped as I felt him grab me and lift me up from behind and carry me back to the bed.

"I love you for your big breasts." He growled as he kissed me hard. I felt his hand creeping up under my shirt. "I love you for your big brain as well," he grinned down at me and I wrapped my legs around him and moaned as his fingers gently squeezed my nipples.

"Oh, Zane." I moaned and ran my hands through his hair.

"Don't tell me you haven't been counting down the days as well." He groaned as he kissed a trail down my neck to my collarbone.

"Okay, I won't tell you that." I laughed up at him and he growled in response as his mouth found my left breast. "Oh, Zane," I moaned in ecstasy.

"Aunty Lucky," a small voice called out to me from the doorway and Zane jumped off of me as if he were a thief caught in the middle of a robbery. I looked up through hazy eyes and saw Skylar standing there with a small smile. "I'm hungry, and Noah is still in bed sleeping."

"That's what happens when you stay out all night." Zane muttered and I gave him a look as I stood up.

"Sure, Honey, let's go and make breakfast. What would you like?"

"Pancakes and bacon, please." She grinned at me happily. "And maybe we can take Noah breakfast in bed."

"Is this a joke? Am I living in a nightmare?" Zane flopped back down on the bed.

"Are you coming down?" I turned to look at him and mouthed *I'm sorry.*

"No." He sighed. "I think I need to take care of myself before I implode."

"Oh." I bit my lower lip. "Sorry."

"Sure you are." He shook his head. "Close the door as you leave the room."

"Skylar, honey. Go downstairs to the kitchen and take out the bacon and orange juice from the fridge and I'll be right down."

"Okay, Aunty Lucky." She grinned and skipped to the stairs. "Can I watch cartoons as well?"

"Sure," I nodded, not sure if Noah wanted her watching cartoons in the morning, but even I was a bit pissed off that Zane and I had been interrupted again. I watched her go down the stairs before walking back over to the bed and straddling Zane. I then planted the biggest kiss on him and then stood back up, as he looked up at me in a daze.

"What was that for?" He mumbled, with a goofy smile.

"That was to let you know that I'm disappointed as well, but that I will make sure we make up for this missed night."

"Well, I can't argue with that." He smiled at me and the expression in his eyes changed from one of lust to one of love and devotion. "You do know it's about more than sex, right?"

"Of course I do." I laughed. "If I didn't know that by now, we'd be in big trouble."

"You're a sexy woman, Lucky. I can't help it if I want to ravish you every minute of every hour."

"Then I guess I'm one very lucky woman." I ran my fingers down his chest and to his boxer shorts and held onto his hardness for a few

62

seconds. "A lucky woman who is sad she has to go downstairs and neglect her man right now."

Zane groaned. "You better go now or you won't be going anywhere for a good 20 minutes."

"Oh, Zane," I sighed, laughing, and stepped back.

"Don't 'oh Zane' me, you little seductress," he called after me as I walked to the door. "I'll have pancakes and bacon as well, by the way."

"Oh, now you want some?"

"If my lazy-ass brother is getting served breakfast in bed, you better believe I'm getting some."

"Zane," I admonished him. "Maybe he and Robin got back together."

"It better be something good, or he is going to get a piece of my mind."

"Oh, Darling." I shook my head and giggled as I walked out the door. I had a feeling of contentment in me as I walked downstairs and heard Spongebob on the TV.

I watched my family sitting at the table eating breakfast and I felt happy, really happy. I was so thankful that I had met Zane and that Noah and Skylar were also in my life.

"Enjoying breakfast?" I looked around the table and watched as Noah, Skylar and Zane all ate the food up eagerly.

"Uh hmm," Noah smiled at me as he reached for another pancake. "You've outdone yourself this morning, Lucky."

"Yes, she has." Zane glared at his brother. "Working night and morning."

"Thanks, Lucky." Noah laughed and smiled at his brother. "And thank you, Zane. I do appreciate you babysitting last night."

"Uh huh." Zane reached for some more bacon.

"Can I have another pancake please, Noah?" Skylar looked up at him with big hopeful eyes. "With syrup?"

"Sure." He nodded and placed one on her plate. "No need to ask if you want more, Honey. Just take it."

"Okay, thank you." She grinned and I watched as she poured about a pound of syrup onto her pancake. Zane and I both smiled at each other as Noah continued on eating, having noticed nothing. It was funny for me to watch Noah adapting to fatherhood. He was a good man and tried his best, but he really didn't know the first thing about being a parent. I realized that Zane was likely going to be the same way, and I wondered if I shouldn't enroll all of us in a parenting class.

"How is Robin?" I spoke the words without even thinking what I was saying.

"She's good." Noah grinned so widely that I knew that they had made up. "In fact, I think we're going to take Skylar on a picnic next week. Would you like that?" He looked down at the little girl, who had so much syrup around her mouth that she looked like she could trap a hundred flies all by herself.

"Oh, yes, please." she mumbled as she attempted to pour more syrup onto her plate.

"I think that's enough syrup, Honey." I smiled at her gently and she put the bottle back down with a small grin.

"Okay, Aunty Lucky." It was then that Noah looked at her plate properly and I saw his eyes widen as he surveyed its contents before looking back at me and making a face. I grinned at him and we shared a secret smile.

"A picnic sounds like it will be fun." Zane joined the conversation. "What day are you going, and what time?"

"Not sure yet, why?" Noah looked up at him casually.

"I want to spend some alone time with my fiancée." Zane gave him a look and Noah laughed.

"Zane." I glared at him, slightly embarrassed that he was bringing up our sex life, even if it was in as covert a way as possible.

"Lucky, if we don't get the exact times we will be wasting a perfect opportunity." Zane winked at me, and I felt my face burning up as I looked over at Skylar to see if she was understanding any part of the conversation. I let out a sigh of relief as I watched her studiously cutting up her bacon and placing it on pieces of pancake squares. "Uh huh."

"Shit, if Noah had been here before we got pregnant, we might not've had to worry about any babies coming."

"What?"

"I said, if Noah had been here before we did the hoo-ha, we might not even be pregnant right now." Zane repeated and I glared at him as Noah laughed.

"I suppose you guys haven't had the opportunity to have alone time, huh?" Noah winked at his brother. "Come on now, Zane. I didn't know you had problems in that department."

"I don't have problems." Zane started and stopped as I gave him a murderous look. "Anyway, just let us know when you guys will be gone."

"Sure, Bro." Noah laughed. "I can take Skylar out to the mall this morning, if you want. Give you guys some alone time."

"No." I blurted out at the same time that Zane said "Sure."

"I'll let you guys think about it." Noah grinned and I shook my head at him.

"I'm going to call Sidney after breakfast. I was hoping we could go and see him later this week and discuss our shooting schedule."

"That sounds good." Noah nodded. "I told you, Betty has a friend that is willing to be videotaped as well."

"The Jewish lady?" I thought for a moment. "The one who was in the concentration camp?"

"Yeah, Mrs. Rosenbaum." He nodded. "I spoke to her and she's very eager to tell her story."

"I suppose she doesn't want people to forget."

"Yeah. What makes the story even more powerful is how she and Betty got to be friends."

"Betty used to be her cook, right?"

"Yeah," He laughed. "She had to learn how to cook Kosher because she didn't really know. It's a pretty fascinating story. Mrs. Rosenbaum taught her how to cook Kosher and then never left the kitchen."

"I thought Betty was a housewife." Zane interrupted, looking confused. "Who's Mrs. Rosenbaum and what's this about cooking?"

"She went to be a cook for a few years." Noah paused as he swallowed some food. "But she and Mrs. Rosenbaum became friends and stayed in contact after she left the household."

"That's a bit unusual, isn't it?" Zane looked surprised.

"That's the point, Silly." I laughed at him. "They weren't supposed to be friends. Everything about their situation should have kept them apart, but it didn't. Their identities as an older Jewish lady and a younger African American lady didn't stop them from developing a lifelong friendship."

"Interesting." Zane grabbed another pancake, and I rolled my eyes at him.

"I'm not sure how you fooled me into believing you were interested in history and making this documentary." I laughed. "You really have no clue, do you?"

"You're not going to tell me that you should have met Noah first again, are you?" Zane made a face at me and then laughed. "You know I love you guys and the Johnsons, but I can't say that the subject matter sends my mind spinning with excitement."

"Philistine."

"Ooh, someone learned her word of the day," he shot back at me, and we all laughed.

"So I'll ask him if he's free next week?"

"Yeah, sure." Noah smiled at me and yawned. "I think I'm going to go get some sleep."

"But, I wanted to play board games," Skylar pouted, and Noah groaned and looked at me and Zane.

"No way, Jose." Zane jumped up and slapped his brother on the shoulder. "I'm taking Lucky out and then we're going to come back and relax before we go out to dinner."

"I'm guessing I'm not invited." Noah grinned and Zane gave him the eye.

"You're guessing right." He walked over to me and stopped by my chair. "Thank you for breakfast, my love. I'm going to go take a shower now."

"Hold up." I grabbed his arm. "You're not expecting me to do the washing up, are you?"

"I thought you liked washing up." He groaned and I gave him a look. "Okay, okay. Noah can help me."

"That's more like it." I jumped up and kissed him on the cheek. "This isn't the 50s, you know."

"Trust me, I know." He pinched my ass and I slapped his hand away before giggling and running up the stairs.

"Don't leave any crumbs on those plates, boys." I laughed as I entered the bedroom. I paused and closed the door slowly before pulling my phone out and calling Sidney.

"Hello?" He answered the phone right away, but his voice sounded a lot more feeble than I remembered it being the last time I had seen him.

"Sidney, it's me, Lucky."

"Well, imagine that. I was just thinking about you, Lucky."

"Oh?"

"Yes, I was just wondering when you and your young man were going to tie the knot."

"Oh, we haven't set a date as yet." I sighed as I sat down on the bed.

"That's not a sigh I'm hearing, is it? Don't tell me you're changing your mind?"

"No, no, I'm not." I mumbled quickly. "It just seems like I have so much to do, and yet I'm not doing anything."

"You're missing your parents, I suppose?" His voice reminded me of my dad's, and I felt a little teary-eyed thinking about my parents.

"Yeah, I guess it hasn't really hit me that my dad won't be giving me away on my wedding day and my mom isn't here to help me pick a dress and well, I just don't even know if I really want a big wedding, but I don't know how to tell Zane. And now he wants us to write our vows but I have no idea what to say. And I don't even know what we're going to do with the babies. Neither of us really has a clue and oh, Sidney, I just don't know which way is up anymore."

"Take a deep breath, Lucky." His voice was calm and soothing. "Remember, that boy loves you more than life itself. That's all you need to remember. Everything else will be right as rain. It'll work out. All you need to focus on is staying healthy for the babies. Me and Betty had no clue what to do when we got married and started having babies. In fact, I still don't have a clue, but we got ourselves some mighty fine kids."

"Oh Sidney." I laughed, feeling less overwhelmed. "You always know what to say to make me feel better."

"Cheer up, Buttercup. Life could be a lot worse."

"I know." I smiled into the phone. "You wouldn't know it from our conversation right now, but I'm really happy. Really, really happy."

"Good, that's more like it."

"I need your help, Sidney." I whispered, scared that Zane was going to walk into the room and catch me. "I really want to find the letter Zane's mother wrote to him before she passed away. I want to give it to him as a wedding present."

"What a wonderful idea." His voice was warm. "How can I help?"

"I need the phone number for the detective that tracked down his mom for Noah."

"Sure, hold on. Talking about Noah, when are you guys coming over?"

"We were just talking about that. I was hoping next week."

"That will work. Hold on, please, Lucky." I heard Sidney place the phone down and I thought about what I had just told him. I hadn't realized how badly stressed I was until I'd said everything to Sidney on the phone. I knew I needed to talk to Zane about how I felt. You still there?"

"Yes, Sidney."

"Here's the number. You tell him how important the letter is, you hear?" Sidney's voice was gruff. "And be wary, Lucky. I know Zane seems strong, but he's still just a man, a mere mortal like the rest of us. I have a feeling that this is a really trying time for him. So much has gone on in his life recently, I wouldn't be surprised if he's trying to figure out how to cope with it all right now."

"Thanks, Sidney. I have thought about that. Me, Noah, the news about his mom, the babies. I'm sure it's a lot of information for him to digest."

"It's a lot of heady information. Better men than him have cracked under the pressure of everything. But, he'll be fine."

"I hope so."

"I know so, he has you, Lucky. He has all he needs to get through it all. Now, I'm more worried about Noah."

"Noah?" I frowned. "Why?"

"Because he doesn't have a support system like you and Zane. He has Zane and he has me, and he has you. But he doesn't have a life partner."

"Well, he kinda has Robin."

"Right now, his relationship with Robin is up in the air. That can go either way. She's a good girl, but she has issues. I don't know what's going to happen there."

"Is that what you thought about me, Sidney?" I teased him.

"No," His voice was warm again. "I knew right away that you and Zane were made for each other. Any fool on Earth can see it."

"Aww, thanks, Sidney."

"Don't thank me." He laughed. "Thank God that you both found each other."

"I will. And I'll send a prayer up that this detective can find Zane's mom's letter."

"That would be the best present he could receive."

"Thanks, Sidney. Can't wait to see you next week."

"I can't wait to see you both as well." And with that he hung up. I lay back on the bed and burrowed my head in Zane's pillow and breathed in his smell. How I delighted in his musky masculine scent, I swear that his smell alone could turn me on.

"Missing me?" Zane opened the door and I stared up at him as he grinned at me.

"No." I blushed, embarrassed to have been caught devouring his pillow with my nose.

"Liar."

"I don't lie."

"What's that, Pinocchio?"

"Ass."

"I'm the ass you love."

"Come here," I sat up in the bed and motioned him over to me. "Make sure you lock the door."

"Lock the door?" His eyes gleamed at me. "Is this what I think it is?"

"If you're thinking you're about to get morning sex, then yes."

"Hallelujah." He jumped onto the bed and pulled me towards him. "Bedroom sex is better than car sex any day of the week."

"You say that now."

"We'll try again in a different car."

"More like when I'm not pregnant, as well."

"That is a good idea. I do want to keep my balls, in case I want to get you pregnant again."

"Let's pop out these twins before we talk about any more babies."

"I can wear a condom, if you want?"

"It's a bit late for that." I giggled as he kissed my face and rubbed his nose against mine.

"I'm excited, you know." He stared into my eyes. "I can't believe we're going to be parents."

"I know, I'm excited as well."

"I wanted to make sure you're okay with everything. I know we kind of rushed everything. Well, I did. I know you wanted to finish school and then go and get your PhD and here you are, having to take more time off school and you're about to become a mother and a wife and now you're also looking after my brother and his daughter. And, well, I know it has to be overwhelming and I didn't want us to rush into any of this. I hope you're not mad at me."

"Mad at you?" I shook my head and stroked the side of his face. "How could I be mad at you, Zane? I love you. You've brought so much light and happiness into my life. I wouldn't trade anything in my life. I love everything about this crazy family we have."

"I'm scared, you know." He lay next to me on the bed and pulled me towards him. "I'm scared you're going to resent me. Everything has been so rushed between us, I don't want you to think I'm trying to trap you to me. I love you with everything in my heart and soul, and sometimes I wonder if subconsciously I'm doing everything in my power to make it so that you never leave me."

My heart broke at the pain in his eyes as he spoke. "I would never leave you, Zane. You're my everything."

"I know, but sometimes I feel like I couldn't live if you weren't in my life, Lucky. You're the blood running through my veins. You're the air in my lungs. You're my reason for waking up in the morning. You're my everything, and I don't want you to feel like you're trapped with me."

"I have never felt that way." I grabbed his hands and kissed him softly on the lips.

"You're the blood in my veins as well, my love. We were made for each other."

"I feel like we're saying our vows." He laughed and held me close. I could feel his heart beating beneath me and I snuggled into him tighter, loving the feel of his warm body next to mine. There was nothing better than this moment. Absolutely nothing.

Chapter 7
Zane

I stared at the computer screen in front of me, and I thought my mind was going to explode. There was so much that went into planning a wedding. I understood why Lucky was so frustrated with planning everything. It just seemed like the lists went on: flowers, table covers, table pieces, guest lists, invitations, rings, the dress, the tuxedo, the bridal party, it just went on and on. And I wasn't sure that Noah's idea was so good now that I was in the planning stage. I had no idea what she liked or what she would want. Absolutely no idea. I didn't even know if she should wear a white dress, I didn't even know what size dress to get. What if I got it wrong? She was pregnant and growing bigger every day; what if I got a dress that didn't fit, that would ruin everything! I sighed as I stared at the screen again. I didn't even know if I should plan a honeymoon or bachelorette parties. What friends would I invite for her? Would she want a male stripper? Not that there was any way in hell that I would let her have a stripper there trying to rub up on her. Hell no!

"What's up, Bro?" Noah walked into the study and I sighed.

"Just trying to plan this wedding."

"Oh, awesome."

"Not awesome." I shook my head. "Trust me, it's so not awesome."

"What's going on?"

"Absolutely nothing. I have no idea what I'm doing. I have no idea what she likes or want she wants. I'm a fucking awful fiancé and I'm going to make an even worse husband."

"Calm down, Bro." Noah started laughing. "You're being way too hard on yourself. I don't think many men could plan a wedding."

"Then why did you convince me to do this shit?" I almost shouted. "I have no idea what the fuck I'm doing. So I'm going to ruin Lucky's big day and she doesn't even know."

"Take a deep breath." Noah plopped down in the chair across from me. "You have time. What date are you planning for?"

"What date am I planning what for?" I shook my head at him in exasperation.

"The wedding, Dear Brother. The wedding."

71

"Oh," I shrugged. "I have no fucking idea."

"No need to swear. Pull out a calendar and let's check some dates."

"Fine." I opened my organizer and handed it to him.

"Well, you're the one who's going to choose it, Bro."

"I have no clue." I glared at him and he sighed.

"Okay, let's see. I think we should do it fairly soon. It's still early summer, it's nice out. What about in three weeks?"

"Three weeks?" I made a face. "That seems awfully soon."

"It's not going to be anything big. You want to do it while Lucky is still comfortable in her own skin. She is having twins, she might have to go on bed rest or something."

"What?" My heart stopped for a moment.

"I mean I don't know if she will, but she might. The sooner the wedding is, the better. Tell her you want to take a family trip before the babies come."

"I guess I could say that, and then see if Sidney and Betty could come as a surprise."

"You going to tell Dad?"

"What's the point?"

"Yeah," Noah looked down and then back up at me. "I don't know how we ended up with the parents that we did."

"Have you spoken to your mom?"

"What's the point?" He shrugged, but I could see the pain in his eyes. "She doesn't exist to me."

"She loves you."

"No, she doesn't." He shook his head. "And I'm okay with that. I have you and Skylar and Lucky."

"You can tell yourself that as much as you want." I grabbed his hand. "But we both know it's not true. She's your mom. You love her. Give her another chance."

"She doesn't deserve it."

"We all deserve it."

"You're a better man than me. I don't want her in my life."

"Don't close the door, Noah. Think about it."

"As long as we're talking about thinking about things. I think you need to call Leeza."

"Leeza?" I made a face. "What does that bitch have to do with anything?"

"I know you don't like her, but she is Lucky's best friend." Noah gave me a look. "She'd likely know what Lucky likes, right?"

72

"I guess so," I shrugged. "What does that matter?"

"She can help you plan the wedding."

"No way in hell." I shook my head vehemently.

"Stop thinking about your own feelings for a moment. Who knows Lucky better than any of us? I know you hate to think that perhaps someone else was closer to her at one moment in time, but Leeza is her best friend. She can give you some good advice."

"Or she can set me up and ruin the wedding."

"I don't think she'll do that. From what Lucky's told me, Leeza is or was a solid friend. I think it's worth a try. Give her a call. You might be surprised at how helpful she is."

"Trust me, I would be very surprised if she was helpful in any way."

"Give it a try."

"Okay, okay, I'll call her."

"Good." Noah stood up. "I'm going to take Skylar out for some ice cream, want anything?"

"Are you sure she should be having so much sugary stuff?"

"Huh?" Noah made a face. "What are you talking about?"

"I don't know, but she seems to have a lot of sugary stuff. I don't know if that's good for her."

"I don't think it's hurting her, Super Dad."

"I'm not trying to put you down, Noah. But Lucky was talking about the three of us taking a parenting class, and I was thinking maybe it would be a good idea."

"So you're already calling me a shitty father."

"Are you being serious right now?"

"No." He laughed. "Sign me up. I'd be happy to take the class."

"Okay," I grinned. "I was about to slap you if you were being serious."

"Wait until I tell Lucky about your violent tendencies."

"Whatever." I rolled my eyes.

"Hey, wait a few days before you make that call for the class, will you?"

"Why?"

"I'm going on a picnic tomorrow with Robin and Skylar." He smiled.

"And?"

"You know!"

"You're not expecting her to come to a parenting class because of one picnic, are you?" I gave him a look and he made a face. "I'm your older brother. I can still slap some sense into you. You cannot expect this girl to become a mother because one date goes well."

"I'd like her to come." His eyes flashed at me.

"Okay, okay." I chuckled. "Who am I to say you're moving too fast?" I shrugged. "I'll wait, but let me know what happens after the date."

"Thanks for your confidence in my dating capabilities."

"Hey, we can't all be me."

"There goes any chance of me helping you plan the wedding of the year."

"Whatever." I laughed. "I can bridezilla you into doing what I want."

"Oh God, no. I do not want to see my brother becoming a bridezilla."

"Get out of here. I'm talking nonsense now." I sat back down and grabbed my phone to call Leeza. I really didn't want to get her involved, but I knew that Noah had a point. If anyone knew Lucky's favorite colors and flowers, it would be Leeza. Girls talked about that stuff. I had no idea what she was into, besides in bed, and I was pretty positive that knowledge wasn't going to win me any points in planning a wedding. I grabbed my phone and realized that I had missed a text from Leo. I texted him back asking if he wanted to meet for lunch, and then called Leeza.

"It's a sunny day in Florida." A bright cheery voice answered the phone and I couldn't stop myself from rolling my eyes.

"Leeza?"

"This is Leeza, who is this?" She purred into the phone and it took all of my patience to not tell her off.

"It's Zane."

"Zane who?" Her voice became stiff.

"Zane Beaumont, your best friend's fiancé."

"Which best friend?"

"Leeza, I swear to God. This is Lucky's fiancé."

"Oh, what do you want?"

"I need your help."

"No."

"You haven't even asked what for!"

"I don't care." Her voice sounded petulant. "I don't like you and I don't care what you want."

"It's for Lucky."

"Is she okay?" She paused. "Oh my God, is she okay?"

"I guess you do care about her, huh?"

"She's my best friend, and I have been in her life for years before you and will be in it for years after you."

"You think so?"

"Chicks before dicks, Asshole."

74

"Okay, Leeza. I get it. You don't like me. You already know I can't stand you. I won't even pretend otherwise, but I need your help. The wedding is stressing Lucky out. I want to plan a surprise wedding for her, so that she doesn't have to worry about it. I need your help."

"Say that again." Her voice sounded satisfied.

"Say what again?"

"That you need my help."

"I need your help."

"Beg me."

"You've got to be fucking joking. I'm not begging you for shit."

"Now, now, Zane. I guess you don't really need my help."

"If you want your best friend to have a good wedding, then you will help me." I was about to end the phone call when she spoke again.

"Fine, I'll help. I want a first-class ticket to Los Angeles, though."

"What?" I shuddered.

"If I'm helping, I'm coming to the wedding."

"It's going to be in three weeks, though."

"Then you definitely need my help."

"Fine."

"Good."

"So what are her favorite flowers?"

"You don't know that?" Her voice sounded shocked. "What sort of boyfriend are you?"

"Save your judgment for someone who cares. I know what flowers she likes, I want to know what flowers she loves so much that she would want a bouquet of them on her wedding day."

"I don't fucking know that."

"What do you mean you don't know that? Don't you girls discuss shit like that?"

"Are you kidding me right now, Zane? We're in college. Most college girls aren't discussing what bouquets we want at our wedding, we're talking about which guy we want to fuck next week."

"You're so crass."

"You know you love it."

"I do not have patience for you right now, Leeza."

"She likes peonies, and roses, and daffodils." Leeza sighed. "She loves the color yellow, and peaches and light blues as well. Don't get her a form-fitting dress – she's pregnant, so she won't feel comfortable in that. You should wear a tuxedo. Make sure that your boutonniere matches her bouquet. It will show her that you thought things through properly. Where's the wedding going to be?"

"I was thinking at a vineyard, in Napa Valley." I answered her quickly, jotting down notes, surprised at how helpful she was being.

"Not a vineyard." She sighed. "She's pregnant, Zane. Use your brain. Napa is fine, but choose some beautiful field or something. Somewhere really picturesque. Lucky will love that." She sounded wistful. "And don't get her a white dress, it will get dirty, get something cream. She loves cream and it suits her complexion."

"Okay, cream it will be."

"I'll look online and send you some links to some dresses she would like. Choose your favorite."

"What size should I get?" I mumbled.

"Well, she normally wears a size 6 or 8, so I'm thinking get an 8 or 10."

"Okay."

"And no heels, get her some cute Tory Burch flats. I'll send you the link. Lucky sucks at walking in heels."

"Anything else?"

"Don't forget to buy her some sexy underwear. Oh, and a garter belt." She giggled. "But I bet that's the one thing you won't forget."

"Funny. Not."

"Get white gold wedding rings, or platinum. Don't forget to get something sweet inscribed on them. I don't have to tell you what to inscribe, I presume."

"No, you don't."

"Contact a church up there and get a priest to preside over the ceremony, preferably Episcopalian, that's the church she grew up in. It's important to her, she'll want a priest there."

"I'm guessing an Elvis won't work, then?"

"I know that has got to be a joke." Her voice sounded short. "I swear, Zane Beaumont, you're cute, but you're a real dumbass."

"Why, thank you, darkness in the light."

"I'm the darkness that's saving your ass."

"I know, I know. Thank you."

"I want to be a Godmother to the babies, by the way."

"Uh huh." *Over my dead body.*

"Let me see, don't forget to reserve the honeymoon suite at whatever hotel you choose."

"Yeah. That's one thing I won't forget."

"What food are you going to serve at the reception?"

"What reception?"

"The reception where you thank all your guests for coming and supply us with free booze and food."

"Oh. Where will that be?"

"That you have to figure out, Handsome."

"Shit."

"Just find the venue for the wedding ceremony and choose a place close to there."

"You make it sound so easy."

"No comment."

"Thanks for your help, Leeza."

"I'm not so bad."

"Yeah, maybe you're not."

"I'd do anything for Lucky, you know." She took a deep breath. "I know you think I'm a bad friend and you know what, maybe you're right. I've been a bad friend at some points, but I love her like a sister and I would kill anyone that tried to harm her."

"So you're going to try and off yourself?"

"Not funny." Her voice was tight. "If you do anything that makes her cry or if you break her heart, I will kill you."

"That doesn't sound like an idle threat."

"You already know that I'm crazy."

"That I do."

"Don't fuck her over, Zane."

"I don't think you have to worry about that."

"Good. I'll be waiting on my ticket."

"Uh huh."

"Oh, and Zane."

"Yes?" I waited for it, the moment she was going to hit on me and show me her true colors again.

"Good luck."

"What?"

"Good luck." Her voice was soft. "What you're doing is sweet, but it's going to be hard. Good luck."

"Thank you." I hung up and stared at the phone, contemplating the conversation we'd just had. I still hated Leeza and I didn't trust her, but I was starting to warm to her. Maybe she wasn't quite as bad as I thought she was.

"What you up to, Honey Bunch?" Lucky walked through the door with a glass of water in her hand and I was glad that she hadn't walked in just a few minutes earlier and ruined my surprise.

"Not much, just going out to meet Leo for lunch."

"Oh." She looked at me with a sad expression. "I was hoping we could go for pizza."

"Really?"

"No, but I don't want you to go out either." She made a face.

"What's wrong, Lucky?"

"I don't know." She walked over and sat on my lap. "I feel weird."

"Do we need to take you to the doctor?" I asked her in a panicked voice.

"No," she shook her head and kissed me on the cheek. "I want to have sex." She whispered in my ear.

"Wait, what?" I looked at her incredulously. "We just had sex last night and then again this morning."

"I want to have sex again." She giggled and wiggled around on my lap.

"And to think I was worried that there would be no more sex for us now that you're pregnant."

"Are you going to cancel lunch with Leo and take me on the study table instead?" She looked at me hopefully, and a part of me was quite eager to take her up on it, but I knew I couldn't flake on Leo.

"How's about a rain check?"

"What?" She pouted and jumped off of my lap. "Are you not attracted to me now that I'm fat?"

"Lucky, you are not fat." I stood up and pulled her towards me. "I promise I will ravish you as soon as I get back from lunch."

"What am I going to eat?"

"Do you want to come with me?" I asked slowly, not really wanting her to come, but not wanting her to stay home alone if she really didn't want to be alone.

"No." She shook her head and ran her fingers down my chest. "I know you need a guys' lunch. Tell Leo I said hey and I'm sorry about Robin."

"I'll tell him you said hello. I'm not sure I'm going to mention Robin unless he does."

"Makes sense." She nodded and then I saw a gleam in her eyes.

"And no, Lucky. You're not going to find someone to hook him up with."

"Who said I was going to do that?" She pouted.

"I know you better than you know yourself." I wrapped my arms around her waist and held her close to me as I stroked her hair. "I'll miss you while I'm at lunch, but I won't be gone long, okay?"

"I'll miss you as well."

"Oh, Noah says he'll come to the parenting class with us."

"Oh, that's great."

"But we're not to book anything until he sees if Robin can make it as well."

"Oh, he's asking her?"

"I have no idea what he's doing." I shrugged. "They're going on some picnic and I guess if it goes well, he's going to propose."

"What?" She screeched and I laughed.

"I'm joking. It was a bad joke I know." I laughed at her expression. "Anyways, I'm not sure what he's hoping is going to happen at this picnic, but supposedly if it goes well, Robin's going to be Skylar's new mommy." I made a weird face and she hit me in the arm.

"You're a jerk, you know that, right?" She laughed at me. "You're so mean."

"I'm mean?" I put my hands up. "My brother has lost his head. What girl wants to become a mother after one date?"

"Zane, let's just see what happens."

"Well, that's what we're doing." I grinned. "Just don't go booking the parenting classes as yet, just in case."

"Oh, Zane." She leaned forward and kissed me and I squeezed her ass. "That's so you don't forget me while I'm at lunch." I gave her ass a couple of light slaps and ran out of the study as she yelped and tried to hit me. I ran up the stairs laughing and Lucky followed quickly behind me.

◦⊷◦

"I'm glad I'm not a pariah in the Beaumont household anymore." Leo grinned at me as we finished up lunch.

"You were never a pariah, just slightly unwelcome." I laughed back at him. "Who knew you dated Robin though? You never mentioned her to me."

"You know I don't like to talk about girls I date."

"But you didn't really consider her someone you were *dating*, did you?"

"Okay, okay, you got me. I know I messed up." He shrugged. "Oh well, she never looked at me the way she looks at Noah."

"Which is surprising. You're a whole lot better looking than him."

79

"I know, right?" He played with his hair and we both laughed.

"Seriously though, Leo. Thank you. This could have become a really complicated situation. Thank you for just walking away."

"All Robin did was talk about Noah." He made a face. "About how much she liked him, but that he lied to her and she wasn't sure if she could trust him. Believe you me, she made the decision, not me."

"I hope it works out for them."

"Yeah, me too." Leo continued eating and I shook my head.

"Liar, but whatever. Did I tell you I'm planning the wedding?"

"You're what?" Leo sputtered and looked at me in shock. "Please tell me that Lucky hit her head? Whose idea was this?"

"She doesn't know." I laughed. "It's going to be a surprise."

"Why do I get the feeling that this is going to be a surprise that doesn't go down well? When Noah brought it up the other night, I thought he was joking around. I had no idea you were seriously going to go ahead with this."

"It's romantic, you chump."

"Says who?"

"Says everyone." I shook my head at him and took two gulps of beer. "Remember Leeza, her crazy best friend? She gave me some tips. She's going to help me."

"The Leeza that tried to hook up with you and me?" He raised an eyebrow. "Don't tell me, she recommended Poison Ivy for the bouquet."

"Haha, I know. I didn't think she would be very helpful, but it turns out I was wrong. She's given me a lot to think about."

"So where is the wedding going to be held?"

"I'm going to find a place in Napa or Sonoma. A nice field or something. Maybe a vineyard."

"Yeah baby, a wine tasting at a wedding. That would be awesome."

"While that would be awesome, it's not going to happen. My wife can't drink as she's pregnant."

"She's not your wife yet, Zane."

"Oops, you know what I mean."

"Yeah," he laughed. "Though I never thought my boy would become so whooped. I never even imagined you getting married, let alone planning the wedding. Who stole your balls and how do I get them back for you?"

"Just wait until you fall in love."

"I thought I did."

80

"No, you didn't. If you thought for one moment that Robin was the one, you wouldn't have given up so easily."

"I miss her, you know." He sighed and his blue eyes looked at me seriously. "She was different. A little feisty and spunky, but I liked that. I liked that she didn't want to just jump into bed. She wanted to get to know me. She wanted to really see if we had a connection. And I screwed up."

"Can you sleep at night?"

"What do you mean, can I sleep at night?"

"It's a simple question. Do you have trouble getting to sleep at night?"

"No, why?"

"When I first met Lucky in the diner and first started talking and interacting with her, she was all I could think about. Even in my dreams. And when I started dating her, I had trouble sleeping. I couldn't think about anything but her. Do you spend your nights dreaming of Robin?"

"No," he gave me a wry smile. "Not at all. Though a certain Playboy bunny did make an appearance in my dreams the other night."

"You're a pig."

"It takes one to know one." He laughed and finished up his steak. "Seriously though, you know I'm happy for you. Also, if you do anything to hurt Lucky, I'll be waiting in the wings."

"Why do I have a feeling there are many men waiting in the wings?" I shook my head and chugged the rest of my beer down.

"Because you're marrying the best woman in the world."

"I know." I sighed. "Trust me, I worry every day that she's going to wake up and think to herself, 'What did I do?' I don't want her to turn 30 and then look at me and all the kids and think 'What happened to my life?'"

"All the kids? You guys are only having twins, right?"

"Well, you know." I laughed. "I'm fertile. We might have a whole basketball team by the time she hits 30."

"Do you want a whole basketball team?" Leo looked at me in surprise.

"Yeah, I wouldn't mind."

"Does she want a whole basketball team?"

"I don't know."

"Maybe that's something you two should talk about."

"I guess we'll discuss it in our parenting class."

"I don't think that's the sort of thing you discuss in parenting class." Leo shook his head at me. "Maybe in a marriage class."

"A marriage class?"

"You know, one of those should-we-get-married classes?"

"Oh hell no, I'm not going to any more classes. I do not need someone to tell me that we're not ready to get married; especially with her belly full of my babies."

"Spoken like a proud sperm donor."

"Leo, you're a cad. I'm going to find you a woman to melt that cynical heart and you're going to understand what it's like to fall hook, line, and sinker."

"It's never going to happen." He shook his head and I stared at him for a moment, wondering if I had been the same way before Lucky? How sad would it be if my best friend never found the love that I had found? I groaned to myself, as I realized I was actually contemplating letting Lucky hook him up with someone.

"You're going to come to the wedding, right? We're going to tell Lucky it's a group summer vacation somewhere."

"Just think about trying to stop me."

"So are you still bouncing?"

"Nah, dad finally convinced me to give the family business a try." He made a face. "Seeing as I'm the heir apparent and all that."

"It must be so hard to be the heir to a billion dollar business."

"It's just not what I want to be doing."

"I understand."

"What about you? How goes the book?"

"It's going slowly." I shrugged. "The day job calls first and Lucky of course."

"How hard is it to buy and sell stock?"

"I do a bit more than that, Leo." I laughed. "But I'm trying to finish the book by the wedding, it's my wedding gift to Lucky."

"Oh?"

"Yeah." I nodded. "She's influenced a good amount of the book."

"Cool, do you know what you're going to call it?"

"Not sure as yet. Maybe *First Love* or something."

"Could you be any sappier?"

"Not really." I laughed. "Lucky put a spell on me and I can't break free."

"I'm taking it this isn't the book about one man trying to take down Wall Street from the inside, is it?"

"No." I shook my head. "I feel like that's already happened in real life. A book about it would be mundane. The new book is about a man who was lost and meets the love of his life."

"Oh, so it is art imitating life then?"

"Perhaps. It's more of a metaphor in the book though."

"How so?"

"The man is lost in the jungle." I laughed at the look on his face. "And the love of his life is a monkey."

"Please tell me this is a joke? Are you writing about beast…"

"Leo, really?" I interrupted him. "No, I don't mean love as in man and a woman love. I mean the love of two best friends."

"Please tell me I'm not the monkey." His eyes looked at me hopefully and I burst out laughing.

"Idiot, I'm joking. The book is basically about my love for Lucky and how she has touched me."

"Okay, so it is a sap story then. Move over, Nicholas Sparks, there's a new Notebook writer in town."

"Now that's just sad that you know his name and the book that he wrote."

"Dude, that movie made me cry." He grinned. "And you better not tell anyone that."

"Oh, Noah, Noah." I said in a female voice and we both burst out laughing.

"If anyone saw us right now, we'd be right off to the loony bin."

"I know, but at least I have a fiancé. I have an excuse for knowing the movie and the book."

"Rub it in my face, why don't you?" Leo pulled out some notes and placed them on the table. "Hey lunch is on me. Want to hit the driving range?"

"Lucky would kill me if she knew I was going to go drive race cars with you."

"You only live once."

"Come on then." I jumped up and grinned at him. "But if I get in trouble, I'm sending her your way."

"Sure thing, Mrs. Beaumont." Leo winked at me and it was at that moment that I definitely decided that Lucky and I were going to find a woman that would make Leo fall to his knees.

Chapter 8

Noah

Picnic basket. Check. Wine bottle. Check. Wine glasses. Check. Bottle opener. Nowhere to be found. Shit, where was the bottle opener?

"Skylar, have you seen the bottle opener?"

"What, Noah?" She looked up at me with a confused expression. "What's a bottle opener?" She continued playing with her Barbie and I shook my head.

"Nothing, it's just a contraption that opens wine bottles." I paused for a moment and then continued. "And wine is something that you should not drink until you are 21, okay?"

"I don't like wine." She made a face. "I had some in Palm Bonita, it didn't taste good at all."

"Yes, it's not good for you." I said with a straight face, but I felt angry inside. I was mad that she had been raised by Monica, someone who would have fed her drugs and alcohol without a care in the world. "Do you want to bring Barbie on the picnic?"

"I want to bring my teddy bears." Skylar jumped up excitedly. "I want to have a teddy bear picnic."

"Well, you can bring one."

"No, I want to bring all of them." She folded her arms and looked up at me with a glare.

"You can't bring all of them."

"I want to bring all of them." She screamed and I stood there in shock. I had never seen this side of Skylar before and I wasn't sure how to react. I wasn't even sure what had happened. Just a minute ago, she had been fine and now she was having a temper tantrum.

"You can't bring all of them, there won't be enough food for them to eat."

"They don't eat human food, Stupid." Skylar ran up the stairs and I stood there for a moment wondering what I should do. I wanted to laugh at her comment, but I knew that I couldn't let her think that her behavior was acceptable or funny.

"Skylar," I called up the stairs. "Skylar, I need you to come back down the stairs right now." Silence greeted me and I walked up the stairs slowly, scared that we were about to have our first argument. I took a deep breath and tried to hype myself up. I was scared that she was going to tell me that she hated me and that she didn't want to live with me anymore.

"Skylar, please come downstairs." I stopped at the top of the stairs and called out to her again, praying that she would come out of her room. I stood there for what seemed like ten minutes before Skylar walked out of her room, with two teddy bears.

"I'm just bringing two then, Noah. So they have company." She looked at me with wide eyes and showed me the two bears: one was the one I had given her in Palm Bonita at a fair and the other one was given to her by Zane when she had first come to live with us.

"That's fine, two teddy bears should be able to get along well enough."

"Okay." She nodded and gave me a wide beautiful smile. My heart melted and I reached down and picked her up and swung her around. How I loved this little girl.

"Can we go downstairs and finish packing for the picnic?"

"Okay. Can I have some teddy bear cookies?"

"Teddy bear cookies? Oh do you mean Teddy Grahams?"

"Yes, please."

"Not right now." I shook my head. "But I'll bring some on the picnic."

"Okay." She ran down the stairs and into the living room. "I'm going to watch cartoons now."

"Okay, Sweet Pea." I nodded and walked back into the kitchen. Part of me still felt that while I had won the battle, I was losing the war. I was starting to feel uncomfortable with the amount of TV Skylar was watching. It seemed to be her go-to activity and I knew that I shouldn't be allowing her to watch so many shows. I wasn't even monitoring what she watched. I was pretty sure that Sesame Street didn't come on 24 hours a day. I went back to packing the picnic basket feeling guilty. Maybe this wasn't the best time to be worrying about getting into a relationship. Maybe I was doing a disservice to Skylar. While I knew I wasn't as bad a parent as Monica, I certainly wasn't feeling like I was going to win any parent of the year awards. I didn't really have a clue and I didn't think that love was going to be a great help in developing my parenting skills. I definitely needed to take the parenting class with Zane and Lucky. And now I wasn't sure if it was going to be a good idea to see if Robin wanted to take the class with me.

I walked over to the fridge and pulled out the sandwiches Skylar and I had made earlier and the Rotisserie chicken that I had picked up at Ralphs.

"Shall we bring strawberries or grapes?" I called out to Skylar.

"Both."

"Okay." I laughed and added a few apples to the basket as well. Then I grabbed the Strawberry Kiwi Capri Sun packs and some Oreo cookies.

"Okay, you ready, Skylar?"

"Yes."

"Let's go then."

"Shall I tell Uncle Zane and Aunty Lucky that we're leaving?" Skylar turned off the TV and looked at me expectedly.

"Nah, I got it. Zane, we're leaving now." I shouted up the stairs and grinned at Skylar.

"What?" I heard Zane's bedroom door open and his loud footsteps thumping to the top of the stairs.

"I said we're leaving now." I gave him a small wave and grabbed Skylar's hand. "We'll see you later."

"Have fun." He rolled his eyes and walked back to the bedroom. I noticed that his shirt was off and I realized that I had likely interrupted something between him and Lucky. Oops. I laughed to myself and buckled Skylar into the backseat and we drove off to go and pick Robin up.

⌘

"I spy with my little eye something beginning with b." Skylar squealed as she ran around on the grass.

"Hmm, what can that be?" Robin bit her lower lip and looked around in an exaggerated fashion. "Butterfly?"

"No." Skylar laughed.

"Bacon."

"There's no bacon here, Silly." Skylar fell down next to Robin and giggled.

"Hmm, blue sky?"

"No." Skylar shook her head and leaned against Robin. I stared at my two girls playing and my heart expanded with emotion for both of them. So far the picnic had been wonderful; it had gone better than I had even hoped for. They both got on so well, it was as if Robin was made to be a mother. She had a natural way with Skylar and Skylar was enamored with her.

86

"I give up." Robin grinned at me.

"Are you sure?" Skylar jumped up and down. "I win if you give up."

"I'm sure."

"I want to guess." I winked at Robin. "I have an idea."

"No, no, you can't play. It's not your turn." Skylar shook her head. "It's a bird. A bird."

"No fair, I was going to guess that."

"But I already said it so you lose."

"But I didn't even get to play."

"Oh well." Skylar plopped down and reached for an Oreo. "I'm the I-spy winner."

"Congratulations, Skylar." Robin picked a bunch of daisies and started tying them together. "I'm making a crown." Robin smiled as she answered my unspoken question. "A daisy crown for the I-spy queen."

"I'm a queen. I'm a queen." Skylar danced around singing.

"Does that make me a king then?" I moved closer to Robin and grabbed her hand.

"Depends on what you want, Sire." She winked at me and my blood boiled over as I stared at the curl of her red lips. She looked sexy as hell and all I could think about was how much I wanted to take her, right here on the blanket. I groaned inwardly as I realized that I couldn't even touch her really, not if I didn't want to scar Skylar even more than she had already been scarred.

"You know what I want." I whispered in her ear, as I kissed her cheek. I was unable to stop myself from touching her.

"I think so, Sire. But I'm just a poor beggar woman. I have nothing else to offer you."

"Your body is enough, m' lady."

"Then take me." She flicked her hair back and kissed me softly.

"Do you know how bad I want to take you right now?" I groaned and traced the lines of her lips with my fingers while watching Skylar surreptitiously from the corner of my eyes. "Next time we have a picnic, it will just be you and me."

"I like the family style picnic, though." Her eyes looked nostalgic. "This is the sort of picnic I always imagined going on when I was a kid."

"Really?" I was surprised. "Seems a bit boring. Soggy cheese sandwiches and ant-covered chicken don't seem to be worthy of a dream."

"It wasn't the food I was dreaming of." She lay back at looked at the sky. "It was the moment, the picture perfect moment of the sun shining on the green grass from a bright blue sky. With two parents laughing and loving each other and doting on their children and playing games without a care in the world."

"That does sound like a perfect moment." I lay down next to her, allowing our shoulders to touch, even though it only sensitized my nerves and made me want to touch more of her.

"There were so many times I could taste my happy ending, but it never happened." She sighed. "I know I sound ungrateful and I shouldn't. My foster family was great. They loved me in their own way, but I never really felt special you know. The special feeling that every child should feel."

"You're special to me." I whispered.

"I know." Her voice was soft. "You've made me feel that. I'm just trying to accept it you know." She turned onto her side and stared at me. "I don't want to waste this moment. I don't want to feel sorry for my failed childhood, when I have you right here making better memories for me. Memories greater than I can even have imagined."

"Let me have your hand." I took her hand in mine and placed it against my heart. "Close your eyes." I commanded her and waited for her eyes to close before I closed mine. "Can you feel my heart beating?"

"Yes." She said softly.

"Each beat of my heart beats for you." I spoke slowly. "I don't want to waste a moment of my time with you. Neither of us knows what life will bring us. But right here, right now, my heart beats for you and only you. I'm not going to lie. I'm worried, Robin. Skylar is on my mind all the time now. I'm scared I'm not going to be a good father. I'm scared that I'm being selfish in wanting a relationship with you while I'm still trying to adapt to being a new father. I'm also scared that Skylar is going to become attached to you and you're going to leave us. And that's not only going to break my heart, it would break hers as well. But I'm letting all those worries go. Because right now, in the here and the now, my heart beats for you. My lips smile for you. My eyes shine for you. And these are the memories I want to make."

"These are the memories I want to make as well." She whispered and I felt her lips on mine. I slowly opened my eyes and saw tears glistening in her beautiful brown-green eyes as she stared at me.

"My childhood wasn't great either." I sighed and tried to erase the image that popped in my mind of my mother. "But we can't change our past, we can only create a present and a better future."

"Our pasts don't have to shape us, I guess."

"No, our pasts can shape us. We just can't let them keep us down and stop us from dreaming and going after what we want. Nothing should stop us from trying to live our dreams."

"Not even failed dreams huh?"

"Failed dreams should make us try even harder to achieve the next one." I grabbed her face and kissed her hard. "Because failure isn't what shapes us, it's what we do after we fail."

"You're so wise." She stared at me in wonder.

"Not really." I laughed. "I think I get it from my brother."

"Zane?" She looked surprised.

"Yeah." I played with her hair as we spoke. "Everything that I am is thanks to my brother."

"I thought you were the brave one, the do-gooder?"

"Not really." I shook my head. "I mean I try, but I wouldn't be half the man I am if it wasn't for him."

"Is Uncle Zane coming, Daddy?" Skylar ran over and plopped down next to me and my heart stopped beating at her words.

"I don't think so."

"Oh, I wish he and Aunty Lucky could have come as well." She reached for another Oreo and I sat up and grabbed the bag.

"No more Oreos after this one. You can have some grapes if you're still hungry."

"But I want another Oreo, Daddy." She pouted as crumbs fell onto her shorts.

"No more." I shook my head, but I couldn't stop myself from grinning. I looked over at Robin, who had sat up as well and she was smiling back at me tenderly.

"Do you want to put your daisy crown on now?" Robin picked up the ring of daisies and placed it on Skylar's head. "You're a real queen now."

"No, I'm a princess." Skylar shook her head as she danced around.

"Daddy's the king and you are the queen. Uncle Zane is the duke and Aunty Lucky is the duchess. And Uncle Leo is the court jester."

"I'm sure he'd love to hear that." I laughed and grabbed my phone as it rang. "Hello, King Noah here."

"Noah?" The voice was sharp and my blood ran still.

"This is Noah."

"It's Monica."

"What do you want, Monica?" I was short and I noticed both Skylar and Robin pausing and staring at me with worried expressions.

89

"I'm calling to see how my sweet pea is doing of course." Her voice was acrid and I felt my heart hardening.

"What do you really want?"

"I'm two months pregnant." Her voice was blunt and to the point. "And I think it could be yours. I want a million dollars."

"There is no way it's mine." My voice was hard. "The timeline wouldn't work out."

"Well, when did you get so smart?"

"Don't call me again, Monica. You've gotten as much money from me as you're going to get."

"Well, I got the money from your brother. You haven't given me anything."

"Goodbye, Monica." I hung up the phone, not wanting to give her any more time to spread her vile down the phone.

"Everything okay?" Robin's voice was soft, but the tension in her shoulders belied her calm tone.

"Yeah, it's fine." I nodded and turned to Skylar. "That was Monica."

"What did she want?" She looked at me nonchalantly.

"Just to see how you were."

"Oh, okay. Did you tell her how happy I am?" She ran up to me and hugged me. "Did she want to talk to me?"

"I'm not sure if she wanted to talk to you. Would you have wanted to talk to her?"

"I don't care." She shrugged. "I forgive her for being mean to me because she gave me the best father in the world."

"Oh, Skylar." I pulled her towards me. "You don't have to forgive her you know."

"Yes, I do. To accept love you need to forgive." She looked at me thoughtfully. "We all make mistakes and it's not for us to judge."

"Whoa, where did you hear that?" I looked at her in shock wondering where those words had come from.

"TV." She laughed. "After the cartoons come on, there is a church program I watch."

"I didn't know that."

"I know, Daddy. But it's okay. I still love you."

"I love you too, Princess Skylar." I kissed her on the cheek and she squealed and pulled away.

"I'm going to go and play now so you can kiss Robin." She laughed and I shook my head as I watched her running around.

90

"You're doing a good job, Noah." Robin broke the silence as we sat there watching Skylar. "You don't have anything to be worried about. You're doing a really good job."

"I don't think it's just me. I think we're all helping to mold her and make her into the person she's becoming."

"You guys are teaching me so much." She took my hand. "You're really making me start to believe in families again."

"I'm glad." I smiled at her and we sat there just holding hands in companionable silence. And then my phone rang again and it was another unknown number. "If this is Monica again, I am going to tell her where to get off." I sighed as I picked up the phone. "Hello!" I said roughly.

"Noah, darling."

"Yes." I froze again.

"It's me, it's your mama."

"What do you want?"

"Zane called me." Her voice was light. "And I need to tell you something important."

Chapter 9

Lucky

"So I spoke to the detective and he thinks he has a new and good lead about Zane's mom." I continued talking even though Noah wasn't answering me. "I'm really hoping he can locate the letter his mom wrote for him."

"Zane needs to mind his own fucking business." Noah finally spoke as we pulled into the Johnsons' driveway. "I told him I didn't want to talk to my mom and what does he do, he decides to call her and have her call me!"

"I think he was just trying to help." I reached over and squeezed his arm. "He didn't mean to upset you."

"He needs to leave well enough alone." Noah jumped out of the car before walking over to open my door. "I'm sorry to take this out on you, Lucky, but I'm just so mad."

"I know." I sighed. "I think we both realized that when you started yelling at him last night."

"I was having a great day yesterday. It was a perfect day and she ruined it."

"I don't think she intended to ruin it."

"She knew what she was doing when she told me that I had another brother and that he wanted to meet me."

"She's just trying to reach out to you."

"I don't want anything to do with her." He shouted angrily.

"But Zane is okay with everything."

"Just because he is okay with it, doesn't mean I am." He slammed the car door shut and we walked up to the Johnsons' doorway in silence.

"Hey kids." Betty opened the door and gave us a short smile. "Come on in."

"Hey Betty, where's Sidney?" I asked immediately, surprised that he hadn't greeted us at the door like he normally did.

"Oh, he's in the living room on the couch. He's not been feeling well."

"Oh, should we come back later?" Noah's demeanor immediately changed to one of concern.

"No, no, he still wanted to see you both today." She ushered us into the living room, but I could tell that she wasn't her usual self. I started to feel worried and fear crept up in me as we walked into the living room and I saw Sidney. He looked frail and for some reason he looked different. I wasn't sure what it was, but the light that usually sparkled in his eyes was gone as he watched us walk into the room.

"Lucky, Noah." He smiled. "So good to see you both. Forgive me for not standing up, I'm feeling a bit peaky."

"Beaky?" Noah teased him. "Are you telling us that you're becoming a bird?"

"Did my nose get bigger?" Sidney laughed. "Come and give me a hug, my boy." I watched as Noah walked over and crouched down to give him a hug before sitting next to him on the couch. "And look at you, Miss Lucky, looking even more pregnant than before."

"I'm not sure if I should be offended by that." I walked over and gave him a kiss on the cheek. "Are you saying I look fat?"

"No, my dear. Just that you have that happy glow about you." Sidney brushed my cheek. "It reminds me of my dear Betty, when she was pregnant. Such a look of contentment. Those were the good old days."

"They weren't that long ago, Sidney."

"Don't fool yourself, Betty." Sidney chuckled. "You and I were first time parents a long time ago."

"Speak for yourself, Dinosaur." She snapped at him, but then gave Noah and I a big smile. "Let me go and get the drinks. I'll be back."

"So how are my two favorite movie makers?" Sidney looked at us both with a proud expression.

"We're good." I answered as Noah seemed to be having a hard time processing how sick Sidney looked. I felt my heart grow heavy. It wasn't just that he looked skinny, it was also that the left side of his face seemed to have drooped and when he spoke there wasn't much movement there. I looked around the room and noticed a wheelchair by the door. What was going on? I didn't know that either of them used a wheelchair. "We were hoping we could start filming next week."

"Finally," he laughed. "Finally, Hollywood will get to see my handsome mug."

"You know it." Noah finally spoke. "Betty will have to fight all the women off you."

"I'm not sure she'll fight them off me." He laughed. "I think she'd be glad for a break."

"How are you, Sidney?" Noah changed the subject and looked at him seriously. "Is everything okay?"

"Of course. Are you trying to tell me I look sick?"

93

"No." Noah sighed and sat back. "No, I'm not trying to say that."

"How's it going with finding that letter, Lucky?" Sidney questioned me. I noticed that he tried to shift in his seat but he wasn't able to. My breath caught in my throat as his eyes caught mine and I saw a sliver of pain in his face as he realized he couldn't move. I wanted to cry, but instead I pretended I didn't notice.

"Good, I'm really hopeful that he's going to be able to find it."

"Good." He nodded slowly. "So tell me more about this documentary. Who else is going to be in it, asides from me and Mrs. Rosenbaum?"

"We were hoping Betty could be in it and I think Noah is going to ask Robin as well."

"Robin would be a good choice." He nodded and then went still and closed his eyes.

"Are you okay, Sidney?" Noah's voice was panicked and I sat forward with worry.

"I'm okay." He whispered and nodded. "Please go and get Betty, Noah." Noah jumped up and ran out of the room and Sidney stared at me with fear in his eyes.

"There's a file in my study. I need you to find it and give it to Noah." He closed his eyes. "It's import..." And then his body shook and he collapsed on the chair.

"Noah." I screamed and jumped up. "Noah."

Noah and Betty ran into the room and stared at the couch. Betty gripped the doorway as she stared at her husband lying limply. I stood there in shock as Noah rushed over to him.

"He's not breathing." He turned to look at me with bleak eyes. "Call 911, Lucky. He's not breathing." I stared at him in shock and the ground started shaking. *Sidney's dead, Sidney's dead.* That's all I could think about as the room started fading around me. I tried to open my mouth to talk, but all I could think about was the fact that Sidney had died right in front of me and I hadn't even known he was sick. I took one step and then the world faded to black as I fell to the ground, with pains in my heart and belly.

Chapter 10

Zane

The sun was shining, but there was no warmth in the hospital waiting room. I felt as frozen inside as I did on the outside. I couldn't think of anything or anyone but Lucky. All my nightmares were coming true and I was unable to think of anything but her and the babies. I had driven to the hospital as soon as I'd gotten Noah's phone call. His words still rang out in my ear. "Zane, you need to come to the hospital. Sidney had a stroke and Lucky fainted and fell." I'm not sure my expression has changed since I heard those words. I rushed to the hospital right away. I couldn't even look at Noah as I walked into the emergency room. I was scared I was going to hit him. How could he have let this happen to her?

"Betty is in the room with Sidney, in case you were wondering." Noah approached me with stress lines all over his face.
"They won't let me in to see, Lucky." I turned away from him, still feeling angry, even though I felt guilty for treating him badly. "They're still doing tests."
"I'm sorry, Zane. None of us could have predicted that she would collapse." Noah's voice sounded pained. "We thought Sidney was dead."
"Rationally, I know it's not your fault." I mumbled. "But my heart can't stop blaming you. I'm sorry." I walked away from him and sat in a chair by the window. I stared at the ground and counted the chair legs in the room. What was I going to do if something happened to Lucky? How could I survive? I felt a tear slide out of my eye. Why did everyone I love have to leave me? What was wrong with me? I never got to meet my mom and now the love of my life was on her deathbed. I felt my thoughts becoming dark and I closed my eyes. It had been years since I'd had these dark depressing thoughts. I jumped up and paced the room. I could see Noah staring at me out of the side of my eye, but I couldn't even look at him.
"Mr. Beaumont?" A doctor walked into the waiting room and Noah and I both rushed over to him. "Which one of you is Mr. Beaumont?"
"We're both Mr. Beaumont." I shouted. "How is Lucky?"
"I don't know who Lucky is." The man gave me a sympathetic glance. "Betty Johnson sent me in to give an update. Sidney Johnson is

95

currently stable. He suffered from a massive stroke this afternoon and is currently paralyzed on his left side. He's not currently awake or talking, but we think he will be able to leave the ER later today and the hospital in a couple of days."

"A couple of days?" Noah sounded shocked. "After a massive stroke, really?"

"This isn't the first stroke Mr. Johnson has suffered from in the last couple of months." The doctor shrugged. "He should be able to go in a few days. Mrs. Johnson says she'll call you with more information when she can."

"So that's it?" Noah looked angry. "I can't see him?"

"At this point, only family members are allowed into the room to see him."

"How do you know I'm not family? Is it because I'm white?" Noah's voice rose and I looked at him in shock. Something in me snapped as I saw my brother in pain, I reached over and pulled him towards me and hugged him hard and the doctor left the room.

"I'm sorry, Noah. It's going to be okay." My voice cracked as I held him. I felt ashamed of myself for the way I had treated him when I had arrived at the hospital. He was my brother and I had treated him like a stranger. "Please forgive me, Noah."

'It's okay." He pulled away from me and kissed my cheek. "I understand. You're worried about Lucky."

"Why haven't they come and given us any information?" I asked him bleakly. "What if something happened to the babies? What if she dies?"

"I'm not trying to be a jackass, Zane." Noah took a deep breath. "But she fainted. That's it. Nothing else happened. I don't know if everything is okay, but I don't know anyone that died because they fainted."

"Are you trying to tell me that I'm being melodramatic?" I half smiled at him and sighed. "I've never been this scared before."

"I know. I'm worried as well."

"If anything happens." I started and he shook his head.

"Let's be positive, Bro." He took a deep breath. "Let's just be hopeful."

"Okay." I rubbed my face against my palm and tried to control my emotions. I understood why they say waiting is the hardest part. I thought I was going to lose my mind, sitting there waiting for someone to come and update me on how Lucky was doing.

"Hello, Mr. Beaumont?" Another doctor walked into the room. I walked over to her slowly and tried to keep my composure.

"I'm Zane Beaumont."

96

"Great." She smiled at me. "If you want to follow me, you can come and see Lucky now."

"She's okay?" I felt my skin start to warm up with hope.

"She's fine." She nodded.

"And the babies?"

"Both fine."

"Oh my God, thank you." I gave her a huge grin and Noah smiled at me widely. "What took you guys so long?"

"We wanted to run some tests first, make sure everything was okay."

"And it is?"

"Yes, everything looks good. Lucky fainted from the stress of thinking her friend was dead."

"He's not dead though. She knows that right?"

"Yes." The doctor nodded and stopped outside a door. "You can go in there now. Don't get her too excited, please. We're going to keep her overnight for observation, but if everything looks fine, we will release her in the morning."

"I'm not leaving the hospital until she can go with me." I looked at her defiantly and she shrugged.

"That's your prerogative, Mr. Beaumont."

"Can I go in now?"

"I'm not sure what you're waiting for." She smiled at me and I pushed open the door gingerly. I walked into the room slowly and my heart sank as I stared at a pale Lucky lying there hooked up to some tubes.

"Zane," she smiled and ushered me in. "How is Sidney?"

"Sidney?" I gasped. "What about me? I nearly died, Lucky. I nearly died when I thought something had happened to you."

"Oh Darling, I'm fine. I'm sure the doctor told you. Everything is fine. But tell me, how is Sidney, is he okay? He looked so sick and then he collapsed. I thought my heart was going to break in shock and sadness."

"He's okay." I held on to her hand and showered her face with kisses. "He had a stroke. I guess this isn't the first one he's had. He's not talking right now." My voice broke as I realized what I was saying. Now I was no longer worried about Lucky, my heart was breaking all over again, but this time it was for Sidney.

"Is he going to be okay?"

"I don't know." I bit my lip. "He'll live, but I don't know if he's going to talk again. The doctor said he's paralyzed on one side."

"I could see." She nodded, her eyes full of tears. "I knew something was wrong. I just didn't know what."

"Yeah, I noticed things seemed a bit off the last time I saw him as well, but I wasn't really sure what. But he's an old man, Lucky. He's not immortal. He will die at some point."

"But I want him to see us get married and I want him to see the babies. He's the only granddad they'll have."

"I know." I sighed as I realized our kids weren't going to have grandparents. "And he will get to see them, Lucky. I'm sure of it. And our babies will have us and Noah and Skylar and we will all love them with all our hearts. They'll be surrounded by love."

"I know." Her hands clasped mine as I rubbed her belly. "They are going to be so spoiled."

"Don't ever scare me like that again, Lucky."

"I won't." She bit her lip. "I was thinking."

"Uh oh, what?"

"Well, I think you should call your dad. See how he is, reach out to him."

"What's the point?"

"I know he hasn't been a great dad, but I think you're being hypocritical. How can you expect Noah to talk to his mom if you're not willing to give your dad a chance?"

"He doesn't care about me and Noah." I sighed. "He didn't even tell me about my mom."

"Give him a chance to explain."

"You really want me to call him?"

"Yes." She nodded. "I do."

"Fine. But only because I love you and I would do anything for you."

"Then get on this bed and give me a good cuddle."

"What about the tubes?"

"It'll be fine." She grinned at me. "Oh and Zane?"

"Yes, dear."

"Please don't try and have sex with me. This is one place I definitely don't want to get caught in the act."

"Okay, I'll try." I laughed and got up on the bed carefully and held her in my arms. I closed my eyes and buried my face in her hair and just breathed her in.

"Never let me go," she whispered, and I held her to me even tighter.

⌾

I closed the bedroom door slowly so that it didn't slam, and then I walked down the stairs. I'd never been so thankful in my life before. I walked into the quiet living room and sat on the couch and thought about the last few days. The hospital had kept Lucky in for an extra day because they had wanted to monitor the heartbeat of one of the babies. I had tried as hard as I could to hide my worry, but Lucky had seen through my disguise. I felt a bit pathetic having her comfort me, when I should have been the one comforting her.

"Ruby Lane will be fine," she had reassured me, over and over. I had wanted to tell her to be quiet. I didn't want her to use the name we had chosen for the girl. Using the name made her too real in my mind and my heart. If anything happened now, it wouldn't just be something that had happened to my unborn child; it would be something that had happened to my little girl Ruby Lane. I could already picture her in my mind. She'd have her mother's big brown eyes and long brown curly hair and the boy, well the boy would look like me and he'd take care of his sister like she was the most important person on earth. My heart fluttered as I thought about holding my babies' hands for the first time, watching them learn to walk and to talk. I thought about my boy having to live a life without Ruby, his other half, and my heart broke. How would he ever be able to live a full life when part of him was gone? I took a deep breath and sat back and said a little prayer of thanks to God.

"Thank you for keeping them safe. Please continue to protect and bless my family, God. In Jesus Christ's name I pray. Amen." I opened my eyes and almost laughed at myself. I was never really one to pray, but I found that now it comforted me. Finding Lucky had given me reason to believe in a power far greater than myself. I opened my phone and pressed the numbers I knew by heart, even though I never dialed them. The phone rang once and then he picked up.

"Zane."

"Dad." There was silence on the line as he waited for me to speak. I didn't know what to say. I wanted to scream and shout at him. I wanted to tell him how much I hated him. How I wished he wasn't in my life. How he was a shitty father.

"It's a nice day in LA today." He spoke as if I were one of his employees.

"I want to know about my mother."

"They say no rain for the next couple of days."

"I want to know about my real mother."

"She's in France."

"I want to know about my mother, the one that died in childbirth."

99

"How did you know?" His tone changed and I could tell he was surprised.

"No thanks to you."

"I didn't want you to know. I didn't want you to blame yourself."

"My, aren't *you* a caring father." I said sarcastically

"You hate me." It was a statement and not a question.

"What do you think?"

"I loved her, you know."

"No, I don't know." I felt anger building up in my voice. "I don't want to argue. I just want to know about her. I want to know about the woman who gave birth to me and died."

"She was beautiful. She loved me for me. She loved you as well. She loved you even more than she loved me."

"Is that why you hate me? Because she died giving birth to me?"

"I don't hate you, Zane." He sighed. "I know I haven't been a good father. I've failed you and Noah."

"We made it okay without you."

"I love you both."

"You never came back when you found out Noah was alive. That's how much you love us. We haven't seen you in months. You haven't even met my fiancé. Oh yeah, did you know, Dad? I have a fiancé and I'm getting married. And we're pregnant."

"I knew that Noah never died."

"What?" My eyes bulged open. "You what?"

"Noah was never the sort of kid that was going to commit suicide. As soon as I heard about that kid Braydon being involved with drugs I went to the FBI."

"And they told you?"

"Let's just say I had something on Special Agent Waldron that convinced him to confirm my suspicions."

"I can't believe you knew."

"I've been in the business a long time, Zane. I've seen all sorts."

"I can't believe you didn't tell me."

"I figured your brother risked his life to disappear so you could help with this case. Who was I to interfere?"

"Thanks for looking out for me, Dad."

"It all worked out well, though. Didn't it? You have Lucky now."

"How did you know her name?" I gasped. "I never said her name."

"You're my son, Zane. I keep up with everything in your life."

"Yet, you don't call or come visit."

"I was hoping for an invitation. I wasn't sure how welcome I would be if I just showed up."

"You don't even call, Dad." I shook my head. "Don't try and turn this around on me. I'm not going to take the blame for you being a shitty father."

"There's nothing I can say to make this better." He sighed. "I don't know what to say, Zane."

"Why don't you start with 'I'm sorry'? Why don't you tell me about my mom?"

"I miss her every single day of my life. Getting with Noah's mom was a mistake. I never loved her. She knew that, and when she left I was happy because then I didn't feel like I had to fake it. I never let myself grieve and I never let you boys grieve and I think my heart is still broken to this day."

"Oh, Dad." My heart went out to him. After what I had just gone through with Lucky, I understood where he was coming from. If Lucky wasn't upstairs sleeping in our bed, I might very well have cut myself off as well. "Do you want to come over for dinner?"

"I can't."

"Okay."

"It's not because I don't want to." His words rushed out. "I'm flying to Singapore tonight. But I'll be back in two weeks. I'd like to come round and meet everyone then."

I paused for a moment and then laughed. "This is going to sound crazy, but how would you like to come to my wedding then?"

"What?"

"I'm getting married in two weeks. It's going to be a surprise for Lucky. I'm getting everything ready for her. Maybe that can be our reunion."

"Are you sure?" His voice sounded hopeful. "I'd love to come, if you want me to."

"Yeah, I do. Lucky will be happy as well." I smiled as I imagined the shock she was going to feel when she realized I had set up a wedding and my dad was there. "She'll love it."

"Well text me the info and I'll be there."

"Okay."

"Oh and Zane?"

"Yeah?"

"Thanks for reaching out. I missed out on your life growing up. I don't want to miss out on anything else."

"No worries." I hung up the phone and sat on the couch in shock. What had just happened? Had that conversation really happened? I stood up and walked into the kitchen and then back to the living room. The house felt lonely without Noah and Skylar in it. I couldn't believe that just a year ago, I had lived here all by myself, thinking I had everything I ever needed. When I thought back to the days when my most meaningful relationships were with women who meant nothing to me, I felt sorry for myself. How could I have ever thought that was a life I wanted to live?

I decided to go into my study while I waited for Noah and Skylar to come home. They had gone to visit Sidney in the hospital with Robin and I had seen them arriving as Lucky and I had left. We all still had heavy hearts, even though everything was fine with Lucky and the babies. Sidney was also physically okay for now, but he couldn't walk without help, and the doctors weren't sure if he would ever be able to talk again.

It was with a heavy heart that I started making phone calls to different vineyards to see if they had a field I could rent out for the wedding. Part of me wasn't sure if I should continue making the plans for the wedding, but I knew this was the sort of occasion that could bring us all together and make our lives happy again. I only hoped that Sidney and Betty would be able to be part of our special day, or I knew it would feel incomplete.

Chapter 11

Noah

"Thank you, Noah." Betty hugged me as we got to my car door. "Sidney didn't want me to tell the kids and scare them so I've been all alone dealing with him. You don't know what a help you've been to me this last week."

"Betty, I look at you and Sidney as my pseudo parents. I hope you know there's nothing I wouldn't do for each of you."

"You know, you're like a son to us. Sidney loves you like you were from his loins."

"He's been a father to me." I teared up. "I can never repay him for everything he's given me, all the advice and support."

"You don't need to repay him. Just come visit when you can."

"I'll be here every week, Betty. You know that. And I will continue to do everything I can. I just want to see him talk again."

"I don't know." She sighed. "He's old, and this isn't his first stroke. I told him to be careful with what he eats." She wiped away some tears. "But what's the point of nagging now?"

"Are you going to be okay? I can stay the night if you need help."

"No." She shook her head. "I can handle one night by myself. The CNA starts tomorrow and she'll be with us 7 days a week."

"It will be good for you to have some help."

"I just can't do it by myself. I can't carry him and bathe him and feed him." She squeezed my arm. "I'm sorry, I shouldn't complain."

"Betty, you're not complaining." I shook my head and gave her a big hug. "You're the strongest woman I know."

"You're a good boy, Noah." She rubbed my cheek.

"I don't know about that," I sighed, reluctant to get into the car. "Call me if you need anything, okay. No matter what time."

"I will, thank you Noah. You drive home safely, you hear?"

"Yes, Ma'am." I got into the car and drove off, with Betty waving behind me. I felt sad as I drove home. My heart was full of sorrow and sadness and all I wanted to do was cry. I thought about Sidney's face as we put him to bed. His eyes were full of emotions, yet he couldn't express them. When he tried to talk, nothing came. Yet, I knew he wanted to say something. There was frustration in his glance and eventually he tuned us out. I tried talking to him, but it was weird talking to someone who couldn't respond.

I felt so helpless. I kept talking and talking, trying to make him laugh, but he just stared at me with a blank unhappy expression. In all the years that I'd known Sidney, he had never not had a smile on his face. He'd always been the one to bring me out of my funk. He'd always been the one to tell me what to do and I missed his words of wisdom. I'd never regretted going to Palm Bonita until now. Maybe if I hadn't gone, I would've noticed that he looked sick. Maybe I could've done something to prevent the strokes. I'd missed out on a year of conversations with him and now he might never be able to speak to me again.

I drove aimlessly, not wanting to go home and have Skylar see me so upset. I was frustrated and angry. Yet, there was nothing I could do. This was life. It was never going to be one smooth sweet ride. I was beginning to understand that. It didn't matter how many hurdles I had already crossed; there were always more waiting for me. I drove into a Target parking lot and stopped the car. It took only a few moments for my tears to come flying out. I hit the steering wheel in frustration, wanting to shout and scream. Why had this happened to Sidney? It wasn't fair. What had he done? Hadn't he and Betty already had a tough enough life? I was worried about Betty as well. I knew she was putting on a brave face, but I noticed that her hair was looking whiter than ever. She wasn't even bothering to dye it anymore. Her clothes didn't look like they had been ironed, and she looked scared and worried. I didn't know how she was able to cope without telling her kids, but I knew that Sidney had always said that if he ever got sick, he wouldn't want his children to know. "Sickness is a part of life," he used to say. "I don't want them to spend years of their lives worried about me. I want them to live their lives and do what they want to do free of guilt." At the time, I had agreed with what he said, but now I wasn't so sure that was such a good idea. His kids deserved to know what was happening to him before it was too late. I would want to know if he was my dad.

I bit my lip as I thought about my mom and her phone call. I hadn't told Zane and Lucky everything about that call. I'd only told them that she wanted me to meet my brother. I hadn't told them that she was dying of cancer. I hadn't wanted to think about it. If I didn't think about it, it wouldn't be real. But now that I was faced with Sidney's mortality, I couldn't stop thinking about my mother. I'd spent half my life thinking about her and our eventual reunion. I had dreamed of our joyful reunion every night for years. I'd been obsessed with finding her, and I had been devastated when I finally met her and everything I had thought was wrong. *Aside from the fact that she loves you*, a voice whispered inside my head. *She never stopped loving you.*

I tried to remember the words Skylar had spoken at the picnic, something about not being able to fully love until you had forgiveness in your heart. And I knew that she and the TV preacher were right. I still harbored resentment and pain in my heart and I knew that if she died before we talked it out, I would never forgive myself. I wiped away my tears and pulled out my phone. I knew that Sidney would want me to make this call. I smiled to myself as I thought about what he would do when I told him. I hoped that it would bring a smile to his face.

"Bonjour."

"Bonjour, comment ca va?"

"Noah?" Her voice was light with disbelief.

"Oui."

"Noah!" She almost sung my name. "I am so happy to hear from you."

"Sidney had a stroke."

"Oh, no. That's horrible. I'm sorry."

"He can't talk." I paused as I felt tears rising and threatening to fall. "He can't talk and he can't move. It's the second one he's had in the last couple of weeks. He didn't tell me about the first one."

"I'm sorry to hear that, Noah. I know he's your friend."

"He's more than my friend. He's the father I never had. He's my mentor. He believed in me and trusted in me when no one else did."

"I have always believed in you, Noah."

"You left." I shouted. "You abandoned me and my brother and then you disowned my brother."

"I was wrong to do that."

"I'm only calling to talk to you because I can't talk to Sidney." I ignored her. "And because Skylar taught me that to move on in life we have to forgive those who have hurt us."

"It kills me that I hurt you."

"You don't get to say that. You don't get to try and make everything okay. I don't want you in my life."

"I'm your mother, Noah."

"And Sidney is my best friend." I felt the tears rushing out of my eyes again. "You don't understand how I'm feeling right now."

"You feel like a piece of you has been ripped out and you can't find the hole to stuff it and stop the pain." She spoke slowly.

"You *don't* know how I feel."

"My cancer's in remission."

"What?" My heart stopped for a moment.

"The chemo worked. I'm in remission."

"So you don't have cancer anymore?"

"That's right, for now I'm cancer free." Her voice grew soft. "If you were calling me because of what I said in my last call, about me dying and wanting to see you, you don't have to feel guilty. I'm not dying anymore. Well, at least not of cancer."

"So you're fine?"

"I'm cancer free, but I'm not fine. I want to see you."

"You made your choice years ago."

"I'll tell your father I don't need the money anymore if that will prove to you how much I want a relationship with you."

"What will you do for money?" I scoffed.

"I can sell the farmhouse. We can move to an apartment somewhere. I'd rather have you in my life. I'd rather Pierre get to know his brother."

"What about Zane?"

"I was immature and petty." She sighed. "I will have him in my life if he will have me."

"Really?" I asked suspiciously.

"I know I've a lot to make up for." She sighed. "I don't want to waste this opportunity to have you in my life again."

"You almost sound sincere."

"Give me a chance, Noah. Let me prove myself to you. Please."

"I guess so." I took a deep breath. "But I'm not coming to visit any time soon. If things go well, I will come next year and bring Skylar, during the summer."

"That would be nice. I can't wait to meet her."

"Yeah, she'd like to have a grandma." I said the word grandma hesitantly.

"And I would love to be one."

"I guess we'll see how it goes." I sat back, feeling content with the way the conversation had gone. I knew that Sidney would be happy I was trying to make amends with my mother. Thinking of Sidney again made me shiver. I couldn't imagine never being able to talk to him again. I just didn't know what I'd do if I never got to hear his advice or his laugh again.

⁏⁏⁏

Robin opened the door and stood there with her arms wide open. I fell into them and pulled her into my arms, before slamming the door shut. Wordlessly, we walked to her bedroom. I tore my clothes off and watched as she slipped off the robe she was wearing. She was naked underneath it and I grabbed ahold of her and fell onto the bed with her on top of me, kissing her hard. Our fingers explored each other and she rolled me over onto my back and pulled away from me and stared at me intently. She stared at my bloodshot eyes and kissed every inch of them, licking the residue of tears from my cheeks.

I rolled her over onto her back and kissed my way down her stomach to her most intimate of places. My tongue found her bud, already soaked with lust and I lapped her up with my tongue, delighting at the taste of her as she trembled beneath me. I closed my eyes as my tongue entered her and she buckled underneath me, with a small whimper. I was glad for the silence, there were no words to ruin the moment. There were no words that could touch the magic of the silence that filled the room as our two bodies connected and became one. Robin was like home to me. I hadn't known her long and we were still in the beginning stages of dating, but I knew in my heart and soul that one day she was going to become my wife. I looked up at her before I entered her, and I felt my heart explode as she kissed her lips lightly against mine, clenched her legs around my waist and then whispered in my ear.

"I love you, Noah Beaumont." Five simple words, but they were better than any orgasm I'd ever had. I wanted to ask her to marry me then. I wanted to get down on bended knee and beg her to be my wife, but I knew it wasn't the right time. When I proposed it was going to be in the midst of a joyous occasion, not when I was still in sorrow over the ill health of my best friend. I loved Robin, but I wanted to ensure that when I told her and asked her to spend the rest of her life with me, she knew it was for all the right reasons.

Chapter 12

Lucky

"**L**et's sing another song." Skylar was giddy with excitement and I shared a smile with Zane as Noah and Skylar started another chorus of "When the Saints Go Marching In."

"You guys aren't getting tired yet?" Zane peered at them in the rearview mirror and then squeezed my knee. "We should be there in about another hour or so."

"Awesome." I smiled at him, before yawning. "I can't believe you surprised me with a family trip to Napa."

"I thought it would be something you'd enjoy."

"It is." I smiled happily. "It's the perfect way for us all to relax after the last two weeks."

"Thanks for inviting me, guys." Robin chimed in from the backseat.

"I'm happy to be included in family trips. I've been dreaming of this day for years." She laughed. "Only I was ten in the dream."

"Better late than never though." Noah kissed her on the cheek and she nodded happily. "Though you really didn't need to bring 3 suitcases for a weekend trip."

"You know us girls," Robin rolled her eyes at Noah. "Can't go anywhere without an assortment of clothes."

"Typical female." Zane threw in and they all laughed.

"So what's the plan for the weekend?" I wondered aloud. "I'm curious what we're all going to do, seeing as Skylar and I can't drink alcohol."

"I have some things planned." Zane's eyes sparkled at me and I knew he was keeping a secret from me, but I decided to be patient.

"And when will I know of these plans?"

"Tomorrow morning." He grinned. "You'll know all about them tomorrow morning."

"I know the plans." Skylar squealed and I saw Noah's hand fly to her mouth and cover it before he whispered something in her ear. I looked over at Zane and witnessed him giving Noah a quick death stare before pulling into a gas station.

"Let's fill up one last time and then we can be on our way again." Zane hopped out of the car and then stuck his head back in. "Uh, Robin do you think you could help me with something for a second. I want to make sure I didn't leave something important at home."

"Sure," She hopped out of the car and then I turned to look at Noah. "Okay, what is going on?"

"Nothing." He said too innocently.

"Uh huh," I rolled my eyes. "I wasn't born yesterday. I may be a little slower to walk because I'm pregnant, but I'm not slow period."

"Lucky, I can't say a word and neither can big mouth Skylar here." He made a face. "I'm sorry, but Zane would kill us if we ruined the surprise."

"He better not be throwing me a baby shower." I moaned. "I don't want to lug a bunch of a toys back home from Napa."

"I can't say a word."

I glared at Noah and Skylar and she giggled as I made faces at them. I hated and loved surprises. I hated not knowing what was going on, but loved the fact that someone had taken the time out to do something for me without me knowing. Only I wanted to know what was going on. I had no idea what Zane could have planned for me. Whatever it was, he had been super quiet about it. In fact, I had only known about this trip for two days. And there was no way he could have planned anything big in that amount of time. Unless of course, it really was just a family trip, but for some reason I highly doubted that.

"You're not getting sex for a year if you've planned something crazy, Zane Beaumont." I hissed at him as he got back in the car. "I mean it, not for a whole year."

"You can't keep your hands off me, Kinky McLucky."

"You want to bet?"

"Hmm," he grinned at me. "I bet you a year's worth of dishes that you'll be all over me tomorrow night."

"Really?" I laughed. "Are you sure you want to do that?"

"I'm sure." He leaned over and kissed my nose before restarting the car. "I'm willing to risk it."

"If you think I won't abstain for one night to get out of a year's worth of dishes, then you are a fool."

"I'm willing to take my chances."

"You're on." I sat back smugly. There was no way I was going to lose this bet.

"Oh, Lucky. I can't wait to see your face tomorrow night." He laughed confidently and I stuck my nose up at him.

"I wouldn't count on seeing anything other than me sleeping." I winked at him and turned around and saw Robin and Noah laughing their heads off. "I don't know what you two are laughing at! Imagine keeping a secret from a pregnant woman, for shame!"

"Lucky, don't try and pressure them into saying anything. I told you already, we're going on a family trip."

"Uh huh." I rolled my eyes. "Sure."

"If I were you, I'd sit back and relax, my dear." Zane squeezed my knee and I decided to take his advice as I was starting to feel very sleepy.

⊛

The sunlight pouring through the window woke me up. I stretched out and opened my eyes slowly, feeling relaxed in the warm comfortable bed. I reached over for Zane and felt dismayed when I realized he was no longer in the bed with me.

"Good Morning, my love." Zane's face bent down to kiss me as he handed me 12 single stem red roses.

"Good morning," I kissed him back eagerly and tried to pull him down on the bed with me, but he shook his head and sat down on the edge of the bed instead. "What are the roses for?"

"The roses are for you, to show you how much I love you."

"How sweet, thank you." I stared into his blue eyes and felt a twitter of excitement.

"I wrote something for you." He took my hand in his and cleared his throat. "I wrote this for you a few weeks ago. I wanted to sing it to you the morning of our wedding so you could know how much you mean to me. I wanted the day to be perfect."

"The day of our wedding?" I asked confused, but he kissed me to shush me.

> *I love you, I love you, more than words can say.*
> *I need you, I need you, more and more each day.*
> *I'll cherish you, I'll cherish you, in every single way.*
> *I'll protect you, I'll protect you, as if you were made of clay.*
> *I'll watch you, I'll watch you, like the sun rising in the bay.*
> *Just love me, please love me and that will keep all my worries away.*

"Oh, Zane, you wrote that for me?" I stared at him in amazement, with tears of joy falling from my eyes as I pulled him towards me. My heart

110

was bursting with happiness and I wasn't sure I was ever going to be able to stop smiling.

"Lucky Starr Morgan, I think I fell in love with you the first time I saw you dancing in Lou's diner. You definitely wormed your way into my heart the first time you smiled at me. From the moment you entered my life, I've felt more alive than I've ever felt before. You've made me complete in ways that I never knew existed. When I wake in the morning, I check to make sure you're breathing before I do anything else. And when I see your chest rise, my own heart can start beating. You're as important to my existence as the oxygen in the air. You're my everything, Lucky, and I want to marry you so that I can spend the rest of my life trying to prove my love to you." Zane then got down on the floor and looked up at me with tears in his eyes. "I've done this once before, but I want to ask you again. Will you marry me, Lucky?"

"Of course, my love. Oh, Zane." I jumped out of the bed and held him to me as I showered him in kisses. "You've already made me so happy. I didn't know you could make me even happier."

"I want us to get married today." He grinned at me impishly. "If you'll have me. I planned a wedding for us today."

"You did what?" My mouth fell open with shock. "Wait, what? How'd you do that?"

"I have to admit, it was hard." He laughed. "Really hard. But I had some help."

"Who helped you?"

"Leeza."

"Leeza." My heart broke as he said her name. "You asked Leeza? You did that for me?" I knew how much he must care for me if he had contacted Leeza.

"Yes, and she's here."

"What?" I almost shouted. "What do you mean?"

"She flew in early this morning. Noah went to pick her up. Along with Sidney and Betty."

"Sidney and Betty are here?" My eyes grew wider and I thought I was about to cry.

"Yeah." He smiled at me boyishly. "I hope you're not mad."

"How could I possibly be mad? Oh, Zane, I can't believe you did this for me."

"I even bought two dresses for you." He walked over to the closet and opened it. There were two beautiful cream dresses on hangers with an assortment of other clothes.

"How did you get these dresses up here? I didn't see them in the car."

"I had them driven up by courier."

"Driven up?"

"I didn't want them to get lost in the mail." He laughed. "I wasn't going to let the post office ruin our special day."

"Oh, Zane. I love you."

"And my dad is here." He looked at me nervously. "I spoke to him this morning. He made it up here last night."

"Your dad is here." I sat down on the bed in real shock. "Your dad as in, Jeff Beaumont is here?"

"Yeah." He nodded. "I called him when you got back from the hotel. I knew it was important to you."

"Only because I felt it was important for you to work things out with him."

"I know." He nodded. "So we spoke and he admits that he made a lot of mistakes. I invited him to the wedding. He just got back from Singapore."

"Oh wow."

"I don't know why, but I'm nervous." He laughed. "I hope he doesn't ruin our big day."

"He won't." I clenched my fist. "Not unless he wants to deal with me."

"You're going to be my protector?"

"Of course, my love. No one messes with a pregnant woman."

"I love you, Lucky."

"I need to tell you something, Zane." I reached for his hand. "I tried to find your mother's letter. I wanted to give it to you as a wedding present, but the private detective, he couldn't find it. He said he tried everything he could. At one point, I thought he had a good lead, but it turned out to be nothing. I'm sorry. I really wanted to be able to give that to you."

"That's okay," he kissed my forehead. "'It's the thought that counts.'"

"I know, but I really wanted you to have something from your mom." I felt tears rushing to my eyes as I saw the tinge of disappointment and sadness in his face. "I shouldn't have brought it up, but I wanted you to know I tried."

"That's why I love you, Lucky. You would do anything to make me happy. You make my heart full, my love. Yes, I wish I knew my mother or had something of hers, but I don't feel 'less than' because I don't. I still feel whole because that's how you make me feel, every second of every day."

"Oh, Zane."

"So are you ready for Leeza to come in?"

"You're leaving?" I asked disappointed.

"I can't see you in your wedding dress. It goes against tradition."

"Oh." I pouted. "When will I see you again?"

"Soon. At the ceremony." He smiled at me tenderly. "The next time we see each other you will become my wife."

"I like the sound of that."

"So do I." He kissed me again and I kissed him back passionately. "If you don't stop kissing me, the wedding might be delayed."

"I don't mind, my husband to be."

"Of course you don't, but I'm not letting all my hard work go to waste." He slapped my bottom and gave me one last kiss before pulling away. "Now I'm going to Noah's room. Leeza, Robin, and Skylar will be in here soon to help you get ready."

"Okay." I grinned at him, unable to stop myself from smiling in complete and utter happiness."

"Bye."

"Bye." I watched him walk out of the room and then sank back onto the bed, trying to comprehend everything that had just happened. I was still in shock. I couldn't believe Zane had planned the wedding for me. I knew how much effort that must have taken and I hugged myself as I realized I was marrying the most perfect man in the world.

◦❈◦

There was a simple altar in the middle of the field. I held the white peonies in my hand and watched as Skylar skipped up the aisle throwing petals onto the grass, looking back at me every few seconds with a huge smile on her face. I stood waiting for her to reach the front and surveyed the beauty of my surroundings. It was perfect, absolutely perfect. Everything about the moment was perfect. The sun was shining, there was a light cool breeze. There were some birds chirping and there was a fragrant smell in the air. But the most perfect part was that Zane was there standing next to the priest with a huge smile on his handsome face, waiting for me. Noah stood next to him looking just as handsome and he gave me a huge grin as I started my procession down the aisle. Zane's eyes lit up with joy as I did a little dance down the aisle, caught up in the music. Robin and Leeza shimmied in front of me as we made our way down the aisle and Zane and Noah laughed as Skylar started dancing as well.

I grinned at Leo and the Johnsons as I passed them and nodded as I noticed the handsome older man sitting in the front row. I realized he must be Zane's dad and I grinned at the knowledge that Zane was going to be just as hot when he got older. I had really won the jackpot.

Leeza and Robin stopped dancing and moved over to the side of the altar and then Zane walked up to me. "You look beautiful." He smiled at me with love shining out of his eyes as he took my hand.

"And you look so very handsome." I whispered back at him as we walked up to the priest. The priest smiled at us both and then asked if we were ready to start. "Yes, Father." I responded and then started giggling out of awkwardness. I felt a bit weird getting married in front of a priest, knowing I was already knocked up and expecting twins.

"God doesn't judge, my dear," the priest whispered as he smiled at me. My eyes widened as I realized he knew exactly what had me feeling so awkward. Zane reached over and squeezed my hand and I squeezed it back, thankful that I was marrying my best friend.

"We are gathered here today, in this beautiful field, to witness and celebrate the joining of two lives. We are here to bring together two souls as one, that of Zane Beaumont and Lucky Morgan." The priest's voice boomed as he spoke and I shivered as I realized the enormity of the moment. I paused as I realized that I would have to remember everything in my mind, when Zane nodded behind us and I looked and saw a videographer and a photographer. My heart melted as I realized that he really had remembered everything.

"Marriage is the promise of hope between two people who love each other sincerely and promise to love each other for the rest of their lives through thick and thin, through sickness and through health, through rich times and through poor times. In this ceremony, Zane and Lucky are dedicating themselves to the happiness and well-being of each other, in a union of mutual caring and responsibility. Zane are you ready to enter into this marriage with Lucky, believing the love you share and your faith in each other will endure all things?"

"I am." Zane grinned.

"Lucky, are you ready to enter into this marriage with Zane, believing the love you share and your faith in each other will endure all things?"

"I am." I smiled at Zane widely.

"Zane and Lucky, please face each other and join hands."

I turned towards Zane and he turned towards me. We stared at each other for a few seconds just taking everything in and then he reached over and took my hands in his. The priest then continued, "No other human ties are more tender and no other vows more important than those you are about to take. Both of you come to this day with deep realization that the contract of marriage is sacred as are all of its obligations and responsibilities. Zane, I understand that you have prepared your own vows."

"Yes." Zane nodded and then he looked back at me tenderly. "I love you, Lucky Morgan. I promise to always love you, to share my life with you, to keep no secrets from you, to tenderly care for you through sickness and health. I promise to always be here for you and our children. I promise that I will never let anything come between us. I promise that I will provide for you during all the varying circumstances of our lives."

"And now you, Lucky." The priest nodded at me and I took deep breath,

"Zane, I promise to love you tenderly and deeply for the rest of our lives. I promise to listen and to talk and to keep no secrets from you. I promise to make you breakfast when you are sick, and to tickle you when you are down. I promise to be your shoulder to lean and cry on and to be your best friend throughout all our stress and strife. I promise to love you forever and ever." My voice cracked at the end of my speech and I could see tears in Zane's eyes as we stared at each other.

"It is customary to exchange rings as a symbol of love." The priest looked at us. "Do you have rings?"

"Yes, Sir." Zane grinned and Noah handed over the bands to him.

"Okay, great." The priest nodded. "As the rings have no end, so your love shall have no end. A circle is the symbol of the sun and the earth, and of the universe. It is a symbol of wholeness, and perfection, and of peace. The rings you give and receive this day are symbols of the union you enter together as Husband and Wife. Zane, place the ring upon Lucky's hand and repeat after me: Lucky, this ring I give to you, in token and pledge, of my constant faith, and abiding love."

As Zane slid the ring onto my finger, everything seemed to become a blur. I repeated after the priest and slid the ring onto his finger. I was so caught up in the magic of the moment that the next thing I knew the priest was saying, "You may kiss the beautiful bride," and then Zane's lips were on mine, tasting as sweet as honey.

"Ladies and Gentlemen, it is my honor and pleasure to present to you Zane and Lucky Beaumont, as husband and wife."

Even though there were only a few people at the ceremony, the cheering was loud and I grinned as Zane and I walked down the aisle together.

"Congratulations, Lucky." Sidney shouted out and I froze and looked at him in surprise. He grinned at me and winked. I looked at Zane in shock.

"He wanted to surprise you." Zane grinned at me. "The doctors think it's a miracle, but he's talking again."

"Oh my God, that's amazing." Tears of happiness ran down my face. "This is the best day of my life. The very best day of my life."

◌❧◌

I lay on the bed in the sexy negligee Zane had bought for me and grinned as I thought about the bet we had made the night before.

"You're a bad boy. You know that, right?" I laughed as Zane plopped down on the bed next to me. "I can't believe you're going to make me do the dishes for a year."

"You're the one that wanted to make the bet, Mrs. Beaumont."

"You should have told me." I cried out, as he started to tickle me.

"I couldn't ruin the surprise." He laughed and kissed my neck. "Now take your panties off, or do you want me to do it?"

"I don't have any panties on." I grinned up at him and he growled in my ear as his fingers found out that I was telling the truth. "But wait."

"I can't wait." He groaned, as I pushed him away.

"I have something for you."

"All I want is your body right now."

"Zane." I giggled. "We have the rest of our lives for sex. This is important."

"Fine," he sat up, looking at me with a frustrated expression. "What is it?"

"Your dad gave me something to give you."

"Okay." He shrugged and sighed. "And you have to give it to me now?"

"No, I don't have to, but it's important. I want you to see it now."

"Okay, what is it?" He frowned and I stood up and walked over to the table and picked up the envelope his father had given me and carried it over to him carefully.

"What's that?"

"It's the letter your mom wrote for you."

"What?" His body stilled and he looked at me hopefully. "Is it really?"

I nodded and handed him the envelope and he held it in his hands without doing anything. "What does it say?"

"I don't know." I shook my head. "I didn't open it."

"Oh."

116

"Open it now and read it if you want."

"I'm scared to." He shook his head. "I wasn't ready for this."

"Do you want me to read it to you?"

"Would you mind?"

"Of course not." I took the letter and opened the envelope carefully. I stared at the handwritten note and my heart surged with love for Zane's mother. I cleared my throat and began:

My Darling Zane,
I may never get to hear about your first kiss or see you at your first dance. I may not get to read you your first bedtime story or get to tuck you in at night. I may not see your first heartache or get to hear about your first love. Or hear your voice change as you grow from a boy to a man. I may miss your wedding and the birth of your children. But my darling, Zane, know that I am always there with you. I am the wind beneath your feet, the light when you wake up, the twinkle in the sky above. I am your mother and I will always love you. If you could only see how much love my heart holds for you, you would never doubt that you are all my dreams come true. I'm blessed to have known you and loved you for nine months and I will continue to love you for the rest of your life, from earth or heaven above. Know that you are always in my heart, just as I shall always be in yours.
Your loving mother
xoxo

I stared at Zane with my heart in my mouth as I finished reading the letter and his eyes were shining bright with wonder and tears.

"She really loved me." His voice was soft. "I can feel her. I think she's always been here with me. She's always been here to protect me."

"She loved you more than anything." I nodded. "I know what she felt for you because it's the same thing we feel for our babies. We love them more than words can say."

"Do you think we'll be good parents?"

"We'll be the best parents."

"We still have to take that parenting class." He laughed. "And the Lamaze class."

"We have so many classes to take." I joined in his laughter.

"I guess as long as we're willing to grow and learn we'll be okay."

"We'll be okay because we love each other." I leaned over and kissed him. "Love is all we need."

117

"Then we're going to be fine because I love you so much that it would fill three galaxies."

"I love you, Zane Beaumont."

"I love you more, Lucky Dancing Queen Beaumont." He held my face in his hands and then kissed me. "Now, it's time for us to have 'let me get you pregnant on our wedding night' sex."

"Oh, Zane." I laughed and then gasped as his fingers worked their way down my stomach and under my negligee.

Epilogue

A year and a half later
Zane

"**D**avid, put that down." I ran over and removed the Christmas ornament from his little fingers. "Your mother will kill me if you try and eat that," I chided him. He grinned up at me with slobber running down his face.

"Oh, Ruby, no, no, no." I grabbed her up as she crawled along the floor and tried to pull the dog's tail. "I'm going to kill Noah."

"Why are you going to kill me?" Noah sauntered into the living room with a huge grin and then he started laughing as he surveyed the mess. "I am not responsible for the hurricane that hit this room."

"Not funny." I glared and handed Ruby over to him. "I'm mad because you went out and got a dog for Skylar without even asking and now Ruby is obsessed with his tail and I'm scared that one of these days Bruiser is going to take a bite out of her hand for bothering him."

"You know Bruiser loves Ruby." Noah blew a raspberry on her cheek and she giggled. "As do I. How are my little pumpkins today?"

"Fine." I shook my head, feeling very tired. "It's hard looking after kids you know."

"Lucky left you by yourself, huh?"

"I don't know how she thought I could handle them both." I shook my head. "It's crazy."

"They're only a year old. How much trouble can they be?" Noah looked at me like I was exaggerating and I just shook my head. He had no idea how much trouble babies could get into. I grinned to myself as I thought about all the fun he was in for, when Robin gave birth the next year.

"You'll see." I smiled at him as he continued making faces at Ruby. I watched my brother with my daughter and I couldn't believe how much love was running through my veins. Ruby Lane and David had only been in my life for a year, but I felt like I couldn't remember my life without them in it. I loved them both so much that I could barely contain myself from kissing them all day and night. Little Ruby Lane with her wispy blonde hair and bright blue eyes was the spitting image of me and David looked just like his mother with his brown curls and

119

big brown eyes. Both of them were slightly plump, with round red chubby cheeks and they were both adventurous. I had to make sure I was watching them every second or they were into something.

"Has Ruby been bossing David around again today?" Noah laughed as he sat on the couch and moved the Christmas ornaments to the side.

"I guess so." I ran my hands through my hair and checked on David again to make sure he had nothing in his hands. "She was telling him something, heaven knows what."

"She's totally going to have him doing everything for her." He laughed and I joined in. Ruby Lane was definitely the more dominant and protective of the two and she made sure everyone knew it.

"Right now, I wish I had someone who was helping me out." I looked at Noah pointedly. "I told Lucky I'd have the tree up by the time she got home."

"Where is she again?" Noah looked around the living room and grinned.

"She went grocery shopping." I shrugged. "And most probably to lunch and the mall and who knows where. She's been gone almost all day."

"Maybe she's been buying presents."

"I wish she would have told me." I groaned. "I wouldn't have minded going shopping while she looked after the kids."

"You're worried she's going to be mad about the mess, huh?" Noah laughed and I joined in. I surveyed the living room and groaned. There were pieces of tinsel strewn all over the floor, with random ornaments everywhere and pine needles scattered on the floor. The throw pillows were on the floor instead of the couch and the room smelled like they were all farting up a storm: Bruiser, David and Ruby. In a nutshell, the room looked like a pigsty and I knew that Lucky was not going to let me live it down if she came home to this mess.

"Help me, Bro. Please."

"Well, Robin and Skylar are waiting for me at home." Noah made a face and I glared at him. "We have lots of plans for the week, so I really should be headed home."

"Don't give me that. You guys are coming over tomorrow night for Christmas Eve, and I think Lucky told me you were staying the night so that we could all wake up together on Christmas Day and drive over to Sidney and Betty's for breakfast."

"I don't know why we have to stay here, just to drive over to Sidney's." Noah made a face. "It makes no sense."

"Blame your fiancé." I laughed and then continued. "Or blame my wife. It was one of their bright ideas."

"Fine, I'll help. Where shall I put Ruby Lane?"

"Hand her to me. I think she needs her diaper changed." I took my squirming daughter from him and held her close to me. She kissed my cheek and then dribbled on me and I shook my head as I laughed. "Keep it up, Darling. If you kiss all the boys like that, I will never have to worry."

"Worry about what?" Lucky's voice carried through the room and I looked up at her like a deer caught in headlights. She surveyed the room and then walked over to me and gave me a kiss on the cheek. "Hello, Darling Husband."

"Hello, Darling Wife."

"Hi, Noah." She smiled at him and they hugged. "Are you responsible for this mess?"

"No way." He laughed. "I've got my own mess at home, but it's nowhere as bad as this."

"Thanks, Bro."

"No worries." He laughed. "I better go though. I promised Skylar that Robin and I would drive her around Beverly Hills so she could see all the Christmas decorations."

"Sure you did."

"Bye, Noah." Lucky waved as he walked through the front door. "See you tomorrow."

"Bye."

"He's such a liar." I muttered as he left.

"Don't tell me. He made this mess and you, Ruby and David came home and found it like this."

"He might have had help, from Bruiser." I laughed as the dog looked at me with sad eyes. "How did we end up with this dog again?"

"Because Robin is allergic." Lucky laughed and bent down and tickled David's belly. "How are my babies doing?"

"I'm feeling pretty hungry to tell the truth." I muttered and Lucky looked up at me with a secret smile.

"Are you one of my babies now, Zane?"

"I thought I was."

"Do you need some special loving from me?"

"Yes, please."

"Well, you tidy up this mess and I'll go and change the babies and put them to bed and then come and take care of you."

121

"No bed no!" Ruby Lane cried out.

"Yes, Honey." Lucky kissed her cheek.

"No tired." Ruby cried and David looked up at me with a small grin. For a second I almost thought that he winked at me, but I knew that couldn't be the case.

"You have to go to bed now, Honey."

"No tired." Ruby started kicking and I reached over and took her from her mom.

"Ruby, you have to go to bed now." I said softly and played with her toes. She giggled and pressed her face against my shoulder. "You bring David and I'll put Ruby down." I smiled at Lucky and she shook her head as Ruby quieted down in my arms. "What can I say? She's a daddy's girl."

"What can I say, I guess she takes after her mother. It's hard to resist your big blue eyes, Daddy." Lucky picked David up and giggled.

"You're a naughty girl. You know that, right?" I licked my lips and winked at her. "You're going to pay for that tonight."

"Really?" She blinked her eyelashes at me rapidly. "Do tell me how I'm going to pay?"

"Just you wait." I leaned over and kissed her. "Once these two are asleep I'm going to do more than tell you. I'm going to show you."

"Maybe after we tidy up and eat." She kissed me back and I licked her lips.

"You sound like a boring adult." I groaned.

"We also have presents to wrap."

"Can't we do that in the morning?"

"I thought you wanted morning sex?"

"Can't we do it after morning sex?" I winked at her. "And by the way, I'm still counting on getting some tonight."

"You're a pervert, Zane. There are kids listening."

"Hey," I stuck my tongue out at her. "You're the one that said sex first."

"Don't say it again." Lucky's eyes were wide.

"Don't say what?"

"Sex. Shit." She slapped her hand to her mouth. "Cover their ears, cover their ears."

"It's too late for that." I grinned.

"Are we the worst parents ever?" She sighed.

"No, I think we're doing pretty good." I smiled at her as we walked up the stairs. "I think our first Christmas as parents is going pretty well, don't you?"

"I guess so."

We placed the babies on the changing table and took turns changing their nappies. "I wouldn't want to be cleaning any other baby's ass right now." I smiled and her and she laughed.

"Me neither."

"Though, I have to say that we need to change what they're eating soon because it stinks."

"Oh, Zane." She laughed. "Oh, by the way. I forgot to tell you, your dad is coming over for dinner tomorrow. He is flying back from Hong Kong on an earlier flight because he doesn't want to miss David and Ruby's first Christmas Eve."

"I guess he's really trying." A warm feeling spread through me. "We really did it, Lucky."

"Yes we did." She smiled back at me.

"This is the first of many Christmas's that we'll have as a family, but I have to tell you that this is pretty much the best first Christmas any family has ever had."

"Mess and all." Lucky nodded and we placed the babies into their crib before embracing in a deep long kiss.

"I love you, Lucky."

"I love you, Zane."

And then David and Ruby cooed their love up to both of us and we held each other close and just stared at them in wonder. We had finally created the perfect family and nothing was ever to going to break us up.

BONUS SCENE

Zane

I watched Lucky as she slept to make sure that she was still breathing. I always had to check she was breathing before I could fall asleep. I think it's because she sleeps so peacefully and so still. It always scares me to see her lying there, almost like a corpse. I only start breathing when I see her chest expand or hear her moan slightly. The best times are when she says my name. It makes me feel all manly and hot. I always feel like flipping her over and making love to her, so that I can make her dreams come true. I'd done that a couple of times and she had always woken up, with sleepy but lust-filled eyes and responded well. I hadn't really done it lately, not now that she was so close to giving birth. I was scared that she wouldn't be able to orient herself quickly enough and she'd feel like she'd gone into labor or something. I had this vision of me entering her and her trying to push the babies out at the same time. It gave me the shivers just thinking about it. So now, I never initiated sleep sex. I waited until I knew she was fully awake; even though sometimes she did whisper my name in her sleep.

I lay back and stared at the ceiling as she shifted in the bed. I felt a wave of love pour through my soul as I listened to her sleeping. It was unlike anything I had ever felt before in my life. Every time I looked at her, I felt the same overabundance of emotion fill me up. I couldn't control it and oftentimes, she caught me staring at her with a dopey look on my face, which she always returned with a loving sparkle and a tender smile. I was about to be a father. I couldn't believe it. There were equal amounts of fear and joy in that phrase. I was about to be a father to a boy and a girl. To twins. Oh my God. I didn't even know how to look after one baby, let alone two. And the classes hadn't helped. I couldn't remember a thing I had learned in the classes. Why did I have to be such a pig? Most of the time, I had been thinking about how to get Lucky to have sex with me to thank me for attending the classes. I'd been picturing sex in the shower, sex in the kitchen (once I knew Noah and Skylar were out), sex in the bed cowgirl style, and maybe even sex in the car again (but not until after Lucky had the babies. Last time she'd nearly made me a eunuch).

I closed my eyes and tried to sleep, but all I could think about was how blessed I was to have found Lucky and how sad I was that my mother wasn't in my life to witness the birth of her grandchildren. I turned over and put my arms around her waist and lay still to see if one of my babies would kick to greet my hand. I kissed the back of Lucky's shoulder and waited and then I felt it. One strong kick right below my hand.

"That's my boy." I laughed gently to myself.

"Or girl." Lucky whispered.

"You're awake?"

"It's hard not to wake up when your husband puts his arms around your waist, pushes his erection against your butt and starts rubbing your belly." She giggled and turned towards me. "Trouble sleeping?"

"I was just thinking about the babies."

"Oh?"

"How we're going to take care of them." I made a face. "I sure hope you were listening in the class because I have no clue what to do."

"Oh, Zane." She smiled at me softly and leaned forward to kiss my lips. "We'll have Betty's help."

"Huh?" I frowned. "What do you mean?"

"Were you not listening last week when I was discussing whether or not we should get a Nanny or a Nurse's maid for the first couple of months after the babies were born?"

"Uh, of course." I lied smoothly; I had no idea what she was talking about.

"Remember in the last class, they said that new mothers who didn't have their own mother or a mother-in-law should think about getting help?" I looked at her blankly and she sighed. "Zane, do you ever listen?"

"I listen to you." I gave her a winning smile.

"When it's about sex."

"And other stuff." My hand found her breast and I squeezed it lightly. "Your breasts are huge."

"Don't get used to it." Her hands ran through my hair. "Once the babies have finished feeding, my breasts will be back to their normal size."

"You can get a boob job, if you want."

"Zane." She frowned at me and I laughed.

"I'm just joking, Lucky. Your boobs are marvelous as they are."

"Uh huh." She shook her head and kissed me hard before pulling back. "But as I was saying, don't worry so much. Betty is going to come and help me after the babies are born."

"Forever?" I looked at her with a shocked expression.

"Don't be silly, Zane." Lucky rolled her eyes. "For the first few months, so she can teach me what to do with newborns."

"Oh, is Sidney okay with that? Doesn't she need to be helping him?"

"He's made an 80% recovery, you know. He's completely changed up his life." Lucky's eyes shone brightly. "In fact, he's joined a walking group now and a cooking class."

"Cooking class?"

"Yeah," she giggled. "He says Betty's food is too fattening and high in cholesterol, so he's trying to learn healthier options."

"I'm sure Betty loves to hear that."

"I think she's fine with it." Lucky kissed my chest. "In fact, she told me it's the best thing that's happened to her in ten years. She can finally relax."

"Oh wow. So she doesn't mind coming over to help with the babies."

"Not at all. She says she would be delighted." Lucky shook her head. "As I told you the other day."

"Sorry, I'm not sure how I missed the conversation."

"Neither am I, Zane Beaumont, because you told me you thought it was a great idea."

"I did?" I gave her a wry embarrassed smile, as I remembered none of the conversation.

"But I forgive you." She rested her head against my chest and closed her eyes. "We can talk more in the morning. Let's go to sleep now."

"What?" I moaned and squeezed her ass. "I thought we were about to have sex."

"Why?" She mumbled sleepily against my chest hair, tickling me slightly.

"Because you've been kissing me and touching me all sexy like."

"Oh, Zane." She giggled. "You are silly." And a few seconds later, I heard her snoring again. I sighed inwardly and smiled to myself. That was what I got for not listening properly. I held Lucky in my arms and closed my eyes before resting my chin on the top of her head lightly. These were the moments that I lived for now. These were the moments of my life that reminded me that I was living a life that was beyond my greatest expectations and fantasies.

⊙⊗⊙

"Oh my God!" I ran to the bathroom and splashed cold water on my face to try and stop myself from panicking.

126

"Zane, the stairs are the other way." Lucky called out to me softy. "And the car is down the stairs."

"Sorry." I called out and took a deep breath. "I think I'm going to be sick."

"No time for that, arghhhh." She cried out and I ran back into the bedroom.

"Oh my God, are you okay?"

"I'm fine, Zane." She nodded quickly, "but please grab the bag by the front door and get the car. We need to go to the hospital."

"Does it hurt?"

"Yes." She grimaced. "But no one said having babies was going to be easy."

"Oh my God, I'm going to throw up."

"Zane." Lucky laughed. "It's going to be fine, but I'd rather have the babies at the hospital and not here."

"Okay." I ran down the stairs and to the front door, grabbing the first bag I saw and throwing it into the back of my car. I stood there a few minutes, waiting on Lucky, when I realized she probably wanted my help down the stairs. "Doofus," I muttered as I ran back into the house and up the stairs. "I'm coming, Lucky, I'm coming." I ran into the bedroom at high speed and my heart stopped as I realized the room was empty. "Lucky," I shouted terrified. "Lucky."

"I'm downstairs, Zane." I heard Lucky's voice and I went running down the stairs. She stood in the entryway with a glass of water in her hands. "I was in the kitchen getting a drink."

"Don't scare me like that." I ran over to her with my heart racing. "I thought something happened to you."

"Wouldn't I still have been in the room if something had happened?" She raised an eyebrow at me and I took a deep breath.

"I know, I know. I'm being irrational. I'm sorry." I shook my head. "I'm just so worried."

"Don't be worried." She grabbed my hand. "I'm going to be fine."

"I'm just so scared." I bit my lower lip. "And I officially suck. I'm the worst husband to be telling you this on the day you're going to be giving birth."

"I love you, Zane. You're not the worst husband at all." She held me close to her. "You're going to be a great dad. The best dad. Trust me."

"I love you, Lucky. You've made me the happiest man alive." I leaned in to kiss her and she pulled away from me. "What's wrong?"

"Uhm, as much as I love you, Zane. I need to go to the hospital. Like right now." She closed her eyes and took a deep breath. "These babies are ready to come."

"Everything's going to be okay, right?" I stared at her anxiously. As much as I felt like an idiot, I needed the reassurance.

"Everything will be fine." She smiled up at me happily. "We're about to become a real family, Zane. One big family."

"Oh, God. Who would have thought it?" I grinned back at her reassured. I knew Lucky wouldn't lie to me. I sent a quick prayer up to my mother and her parents to look after her and we quickly got into the car and drove to the hospital.

We arrived at the emergency room about 20 minutes later and I parked illegally in front of the doors.

"Zane, I don't think this is the right entrance." Lucky made a face while holding her stomach and I ignored her.

"Wait here." I hurried out if the car and ran into the hospital. "I need a wheelchair." I screamed at a nurse walking past me. "Where are the wheelchairs?" She gave me a look, nodded to the side and kept on walking. *Incompetent!* I glared at her and ran to the desk.

"I need a wheelchair and a doctor STAT." I shouted at the nurse behind the desk.

"What seems to be the issue, Sir?" She stared at me and I took a deep breath, before I started shouting.

"My wife is about to have a baby and she needs to see a doctor right away."

"Did she cut her hand off?" She didn't blink. "Is she bleeding profusely? Does she have a pre-existing condition?"

"What?" I shook my head confused.

"Sir, this is the emergency room." She looked at the nurse next to her and rolled her eyes. "We deal with emergencies, not pregnant women and their overzealous husbands."

"I'm not overzealous." I argued back at her, but took a step back. "Where do I go then?"

"Go to general intake, Sir. They will get your wife to the maternity ward. Have you called her doctor?"

"What doctor?" I blinked.

"The one that's going to deliver the baby, unless you're planning on doing it?"

"Oh. No." I made a face. "I gotta go." I ran back to the front of the emergency room and back into the car. "Hey, this is the wrong place."

"I tried to tell you that, Zane." Lucky shook her head and I bit my lip. "Sorry."

"Let's park." She groaned and held her stomach again as she closed her eyes.

"What's wrong?" I looked at her worried.

"Are you going to keep asking me that?" She groaned. "I'm having a baby, actually I'm having two babies and I feel like I'm carrying twin elephants, who are dying to pop out of me."

"Oh, it hurts huh?"

"Yes, Zane. It hurts. So please hurry up, so I can get these babies out of me before I strangle you."

"No need to get violent." I made a face at her and she just glared at me. I parked quickly and she held onto my arm as I opened the door to get her bag. Uh oh, I thought as I looked at the bag in the backseat. "Hey, I gotta tell you something."

"Yeah." She whimpered.

"I brought the wrong bag." I said softly, hoping she wouldn't hear me.

"What do you mean?" She opened her eyes and stared at me.

"I kinda brought my gym bag by mistake. They were both next to the front door and I wasn't paying attention."

"What did I tell you about leaving your gym bag by the front door?" She groaned. "It's fine. Just call Noah when we get to a room."

"I think he and Skylar are spending the weekend at Robin's place."

"Zane, you know I love you, right? But, you are really being an idiot. I don't care if he's spending the next year at Robin's. You tell him to go home and get my bag and bring it, do you hear me?"

"Yes, Ma'am." My heart started beating fast as we walked slowly to the main entrance. I'd never seen Lucky act like this before and I was hoping that her attitude wasn't going to stay this surly after she had the babies.

"Can you walk a bit slower, please?" She snapped at me and I turned to her with a smile.

"Do you want to have a quickie to get you in a better mood?" I joked and laughed, but she didn't seem to get the joke as she rolled her eyes and ignored me. "I guess that's a no."

"Zane, you'll be lucky if I ever sleep with you again."

"What?" I stopped still. "You're joking right?"

"What do you think?" She gave me one look and I started walking again. I was thinking about asking the doctors if there was anything they could give her to stop her from being so bitchy, though I wasn't sure I wanted her to hear me ask that.

"Oh, Zane." She cried and squeezed my hand. "It really hurts."

"I'm sorry." I kissed her cheek. "I wish I could take some of the pain from you."

"You're so sweet." She caressed my cheek and smiled. "I love you."

"I love you, too." I smiled at her, feeling less worried. Maybe she wasn't going to stay a bitch for very long.

"Having a baby?" A nurse walked up to us and I nodded. "How long are the contractions?"

"Sorry what?" I stuttered, feeling awful. I had messed around in the Lamaze classes so much that I really wasn't sure what I should know.

"Contractions?" The nurse repeated slowly. "How far apart are they?

"4 minutes." Lucky spoke up before I could continue looking like an idiot.

"Okay, let's get you to a room." The nurse handed me a clipboard. "Fill this out, please."

"Okay." I could fill out paperwork easily. This was up my alley.

"Don't forget to call Noah." Lucky looked at me and I nodded. "And can you go back to the car and get my purse, please? I left it by mistake."

"Okay." I nodded. "I'll go now. I'll be right back."

"It's okay, Darling. Take a breath." Lucky grabbed my hands. "Take a deep breath."

I did as she said and took a deep breath and she smiled. "Calm down, Zane. It'll be fine."

"I'm trying." I grabbed her face and kissed her slowly and passionately. "That's to stop you from looking at any other men while I go the car."

"As if." she grinned.

"You never know, some hot doctor may try and hit on you." I grinned. "He'll see you looking all beautiful and think he hit the jackpot."

"I'm not sure pregnant with twins is the jackpot any man wants to hit."

"You never know." I laughed. "I think it's a billion dollar jackpot."

"And that's why I love you." She grinned and then hit me in the arm. "Go and do those tasks and then come meet me in the room."

"Yes, Boss." I laughed and hurried out of the hospital and quickly pulled my phone out as I ran to the car.

"Hello?" Noah sounded like he had just woken up.

"Get your fat ass out of bed." I yelled into the phone. "Lucky and I are at the hospital."

"Oh my God, is everything okay?"

"No." I shouted, and then lowered my voice. "Well, yes, it's fine. Lucky's just having the babies and I brought the wrong bag with me so I need you to go home and pick it up."

"Sucker." Noah laughed. "Trust you to bring the wrong bag."

"Whatever, just go and get it, okay?"

"Can I bring Skylar and Robin with me to the hospital?"

"Yeah, yeah, sure." I hung up the phone as I opened the passenger car door and saw an envelope on the seat with my name on it. I paused as I stared at it and opened it gingerly. There was a letter inside the envelope and I started to read it carefully, a wide smile spreading over my face.

"To my dearest Zane,

Take one, no, five deep breathes and calm down. I know that right now, you are most probably freaking out and very likely getting on my nerves. But my darling, please don't worry. This is a joyous occasion for us. This is the day we're going to meet our babies. Our 'mini-me's. The children born of our love. Because no matter how much pain I go through today and no matter how many times I glare at you or complain, I wouldn't have it any other way. I love these babies, Zane. I love that our love has brought us to this moment. These babies are going to be so loved, by you and by me, and we are going to give them the best life possible. They are going to want for nothing because we will shower them with love and affection and they will see how much their parents love each other. Take one more deep breath, my love. This is a time for us to rejoice and be happy. We've been blessed. Really and truly blessed. We found each other and we're having two beautiful babies. Only think positive thoughts, my love. Banish the hidden demons from your mind. Come back into that room with a big smile and no worry. I love you and always will.

Your darling, Lucky
XOXO

I felt tears falling from my eyes as I reread her letter and leaned against the car. I couldn't quite believe how at ease her letter had made me or how loved. That she had taken the time out to write me such a letter meant the world to me. My heart expanded with love for Lucky and I quickly grabbed her purse, locked the door and ran back to the hospital. I had to see her. I had to be there for her 100%. She was my wife, my darling, and I needed to be her rock. I was ready to be the man she wanted and needed. I hurried back to find her, with determination and courage in my heart. I wasn't going to let her see my worries anymore.

⚜

"Okay push," the nurse commanded Lucky, who was screaming and yelling in pain. I stood there next to her and tried to keep a calm face, though it was hard as hell. Lucky had yelled at me more than a few times and I was starting to feel sick. I reached over to grab her hand, but she pulled it away from me as she groaned again.

"Okay, I can see the first head," said the doctor, who was sitting in between my wife's legs. "Want to see, Mr. Beaumont?"

"Uh, sure." I nodded feebly and walked to stand next to him. I looked at Lucky's spread legs and swallowed again. I started to feel woozy and I clenched my right fist. *Oh, God, I'm going to faint* is all I could keep thinking.

"Push," the doctor commanded, and I watched Lucky close her eyes and push while grunting. I stared between her legs again and I wondered how the babies were going to get through. I thought back to when I made love to her. Her walls had felt pretty tight on me and I wasn't that big. I mean, I was above average sized down there, but I certainly wasn't as big as a baby. How were two babies going to pass through there? Oh shit, I wanted to tell the doctor that maybe it was time to do a C-Section. Lucky hadn't been with that many guys and so maybe she wasn't really going to be able to push two footballs through.

"You got it, Lucky. One more long push," the nurse said sweetly. I tried not to roll my eyes. Who was she fooling? One more push wasn't going to do anything. "There you go," the nurse encouraged Lucky, and my eyes nearly popped out when I saw a baby's head coming through my wife's vagina. "Keep going, Lucky," the nurse said excitedly. "The first one is nearly out."

Lucky screamed and I watched as she gripped the sheets and pushed. My mouth dropped open as the baby continued coming out and then everything seemed to happen in a flash. The doctor was doing something and then the nurse was doing something and before I knew it, I heard.

"You have a daughter, Mr. and Mrs. Beaumont."

My heart stopped as I looked at the blood-covered piece of flesh that all of a sudden started to scream. I looked at Lucky and she beamed at me angelically. "Ruby Lane is here." She smiled at me and I felt tears falling down from my eyes for the second time that day.

"Oh my God. We have a daughter." I grinned back at her and quickly walked over to her to give her a quick kiss. "We have a daughter." I whispered again, this time against her lips.

"Sorry to interrupt you both, but we have one more to go." The nurse laughed. "And he seems like he is eager to join his sister. Push, Lucky." I held my hand out to her and this time she took it and smiled at me.

"Second round." I smiled down at her and she laughed.

"I don't know if we're having any more babies after this." She grinned and I laughed before wiping the sweat off of her face with a towel.

"Let's talk about that again in a few weeks." I laughed. "I told you I wanted a baseball team."

"Then you better go and coach little league or something." She smiled and then started groaning as she pushed and squeezed my hand. I tried to hide my grimaces as her fingers tightened on my palm. I knew it wouldn't be cool if I started groaning from the pressure she was placing on my hand as she was pushing out my kid.

"You got this, Lucky." I smiled at her, but she ignored me and pushed.

"Good girl, Lucky. Looks like this guy wants to come quickly." The doctor smiled at us and I smiled back at him weakly.

"Ruby Lane is a healthy 6 pounds and 2 ounces." The nurse grinned and held up my baby girl, who looked so much more beautiful without the blood all over her head. "And she's already got a full head of silky blonde hair."

"She's gorgeous." I couldn't believe the overwhelming feeling of love that had taken over my heart. I also couldn't stop grinning as I stared at Ruby Lane, even though Lucky was still squeezing my hand hard.

"Oh my God!" Lucky screamed and I could see the doctor's hands reach up to help get my son out. I stood there staring at Lucky and reached down to brush her wet hair away from her eyes. "Thank you." She mumbled up at me and then continued pushing for what seemed like ages but was really only about ten minutes.

"Congratulations, Mr. and Mrs. Beaumont, you are now the parents of a beautiful baby boy." The doctor grinned at me and I watched as the nurse took him and cut the umbilical cord. "Ooh, looks like little Ruby Lane was doing all the eating." She laughed as she took held up the little crying boy in her hands. "He looks like he's a whole pound less than her."

"Oh, no." My face went white. "Is he okay?"

"Don't worry, Mr. Beaumont." She smiled at me. "I'm sure he's fine. Of course, we'll run all the tests to make sure, but as of right now, everything looks great. Do we have a name for Ruby Lane's brother?"

I stared at, Lucky and she smiled at me, with sparkling eyes. "You choose, Honey."

"What about David?" I looked at her. "It's a strong name, for a small boy."

"You mean, like David and Goliath?"

"Yes." I laughed. "You always know what I'm thinking."

"It's a great name." She nodded and I looked at the nurse.

"Then we shall call him David. David and Ruby Lane Beaumont."

"Beautiful names for beautiful kids." She smiled at us. "You'll be able to hold them both in just a minute." She cleaned David off and wrote some information down before handing us the babies. She gave David to Lucky and then handed Ruby Lane over to me gently.

"Here's your daughter, Mr. Beaumont."

"Thank you." My voice sounded choked and I held on to Ruby Lane carefully, glancing down at her little screwed up face. Once again, I was overwhelmed with the feeling of love that I felt as I stared at her. "I love you, Ruby." I whispered as I held her tight. I could barely believe the feeling of contentment and peace that I felt as I stared at her. She was beautiful and she was my daughter. I looked over at Lucky and David and my heart expanded even more as I watched her kiss his cheek gingerly. This was my family. This was what love was all about. This was what life was all about. There was nothing that could top this moment. Absolutely nothing.

"I love you, Lucky." I heard my voice crack as I spoke to her, but I wasn't embarrassed or ashamed. "Thank you for giving me this perfect family."

"Remember that when you're waking up to change their diapers." She grinned at me, but her eyes conveyed the same emotion that I felt. I knew she was overwhelmed with the love and emotion she was feeling. This was our moment and time. We were truly a family now. I smiled to myself as I thought about how blessed I was. The only thing I hoped for now was for Lucky to decide she wanted more kids and lots of practice making more kids because I knew I could definitely get used to this feeling.

Thank you for purchasing a J. S. Cooper book. If you enjoyed it, please think about leaving a review and recommending it to a friend. You can see a list of all my books on my website here!

Please join my MAILING LIST to be notified of new releases and teasers. You can also join me on my Facebook page here.

I love to hear from readers so feel free to send me an email at jscooperauthor@gmail.com at any time.

List of J. S. Cooper Books

Scarred
Healed
The Last Boyfriend
The Last Husband
Before Lucky
The Other Side of Love
Zane & Lucky's First Christmas
Crazy Beautiful Love
The Ex Games 1, 2 and 3
The Private Club 1, 2 and 3